About the Author

Dave worked for nearly twenty-five years in the health and social care and charity sector. After being dismissed following workplace bullying and lack of understanding of his autism, Dave won a legal case against his former employers, a large national care charity. The case received much press attention. Subsequently, Dave set himself up as an inclusion and equalities campaigner, and volunteer for causes such as workplace bullying, autism awareness, mental health, safeguarding and animal welfare. Dave is also a leading advocate of rewilding, environmental issues and a voice for unpaid carers.

The Secret Wild Wolves
of Britain

Dave Gregson

The Secret Wild Wolves of Britain

Olympia Publishers

London

www.olympiapublishers.com

OLYMPIA PAPERBACK EDITION

A CIP catalogue record for this title is available from the British Library.

ISBN: 978-1-80074-839-2

This is a work of fiction.
Names, characters, places and incidents originate from the writer's imagination. Any
resemblance to actual persons, living or dead, is purely coincidental.

First Published in 2023

Olympia Publishers
Tallis House
2 Tallis Street
London
EC4Y 0AB

Printed in Great Britain

Dedication

To my father, Terence Gregson, the best storyteller of all time and who taught me all I needed to learn about the art of storytelling.

Acknowledgements

Thanks to all the team at Olympia Publishers for their excellent and professional services. Special thanks to Declan Morton for his outstanding contribution to this project and special knowledge of the subject. Also, to Aimee Youles and CRS Editorial for their editorial and proofreading expertise, illustrator Samuel Batley, novelist Jeffrey Archer and his PA Alison Prince, George Galloway and Brooke Kinsella MBE. A huge thanks to my parents, and to John, Beth and Esme, Catherine, Stu, and all my friends and family, my two cats and, of course, all my readers.

TABLE OF CONTENTS

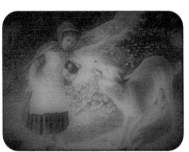

A Troubled History and a New Beginning

The worry of the unknown was what always seemed to drive the humans to fear us wolves, hence the appearance of wolves as black beasts or creatures from hell in so many different forms of legend and folklore.

Just after the end of the last glacial ice age, as the ice retreated and the sea levels rose, the island of Great Britain was formed.

Our populations were plentiful and vast forests covered the majority of the island. We shared the forests with a host of animals, both prey and rivals for food. Even the brown bear slugged heavily around the island in the early years, but they were few in numbers and quickly became extinct before the tenth century.

Humans arrived as hunter-gatherers and we lived side by side for a long time. Our natural attributes and intelligence even allowed man to domesticate early wolves for companionship and protection.

Early records and ancient carvings tell how tribespeople used the skin of wolves to give them powers, and how the wolf was revered as man's brother and fellow hunter-gatherer. Wolves were a symbol of strength and even dignity. This soon changed.

Wolves howl to make contact with each other and they can be, albeit not exclusively, nocturnal. The wolf howl was heard with fear, especially when it coincided with a full moon. For humans, the night was dark and scary, where monsters dwelled in the unconsciousness of the unknown. The unknown had always equated to fear and terror in human history.

The advent of farming and agriculture led to humans deforesting much of Britain. Forests were often seen as dark and dangerous places where evil lurked. Travellers were warned to stay clear of these dark, mystical labyrinths where all kinds of danger lurked: savages, bandits and wolves.

Medieval humans were frequently in open conflict with each other, fighting endless wars. Often, we would feed on the dead of the battlefield until our numbers increasingly dwindled, and we endeavoured, more than anything, to avoid contact with the island's human population.

Kings and queens often ordered the total destruction of all wolves in their respective kingdoms and lands, with large bounties on offer to carry out this task. Servants were frequently employed specifically as official "wolf hunters".

Wolves formed social groups and hunted in packs with an organised hierarchy, shared parenting duties and a structure from alpha to omega. When humans started killing wolves indiscriminately, the hierarchy was thrown into turmoil and packs broke up. Young cubs frequently starved to death and lone wolves roamed the land in desperation, without mates, structure and the ability to hunt properly, wandering into territories of man's domestic livestock. Eventually, the wolves were killed, starved to death or succumbed to disease, lying down to quietly die underground or in a remote cave.

Despite stories of wolves saving humans being woven into folklore – such as Romulus and Remus being suckled by wolves; cases of wolves saving humans including a well known tale of a priest in Ireland who was protected from attack by feral beasts by a lone wild wolf– they got little reprieve.

The era of legends of human shapeshifters, lycanthropy and other so-called old wives' tales further enhanced the view of wolves being evil. Other animals such as wild cats, crows, black domestic cats, wild boar and even hedgehogs also suffered demonisation in the witchcraft hysteria, but never to the same degree as *Canis lupus* or the grey wolf.

When woodland was cleared, we had conflicts with the new practice of farming and keeping domesticated animals as livestock. We were happier with hunting deer and wild boar and wished to keep away from man, but we couldn't.

In Anglo-Saxon times, huge bounties were paid to hunt and kill us. All counties had their respective wolf hunters and sometimes penal servitude demanded a provision of wolf tongues as repentance for crimes. It's tragic that the breed of wolfhounds used to hunt us down and kill us were originally bred from our own ancestors.

English wolves, it was historically written, were more often trapped than killed. Indeed, in the Peak District, official wolf hunters would set traps to capture the adult wolves, then steal into the forest to kill the wolf cubs.

We managed to secrete ourselves away in England to the more remote areas of the north and the forests of Bowland in Lancashire. However, it was only a temporary reprieve. The advent of new, destructive weapons such as the musket sealed our fate, and huge forests such as those of Bowland were cleared and burned, or used by man for his developing industries. One of the missions of the clearing of the forests was to remove habitats where we were able to live.

In our sojourn in England, we witnessed many conflicts in which man fought each other and the systems of humans changed. There was no longer room for us wolves.

Other large native animals such as the beaver, wild boar and lynx were gone by the time we left England and Wales and retreated north to Scotland. Medieval banquets, coats of arms and art and literature promoted hunting of the wild boar and also brought about its extinction as a native species. The last native boar lived nocturnally in the north of England until the eighteenth century. We hear and sense that the wild boar has returned and an ancient knowledge and familiarity provides evidence of its presence today, as we venture above ground, but more of that to come.

Our British population of native wolves found solace and refuge in the great glens and forests of Scotland and for some time we felt safer; we had retreated into the most isolated areas and dark forests and our prey – deer – were in abundance.

Disaster was to strike again though for the British wolf. The Caledonian forests were savagely chopped down and burned; a reason for this was to prevent such forests providing cover for wolves. This was in

17

the seventeenth century. It became the talk of legend about when the last wild British wolf was killed.

Some records say it was 1680; another tale tells of a famous incident where the alleged last wolf was killed near Inverness by Old Man Findhorn in 1743 and the severed head brought back as a souvenir. Many roadside stones and runic-type symbols pay homage to the slaying of the last wild wolf in Britain. We know our Irish cousins survived until the last recorded wild wolf was shot in County Carlow in 1786.

One or two individuals died a lonely death on the wastes of Cannock Moor in the 1760s. A natural survey reported that by 1769 there were no wolves left in Great Britain.

So begins our story of survival. Yes, it's true that by the 1760s a tiny few of us survived by encamping in the most remote parts of the Scottish Highlands. Keeping out of all trace of human existence, the windswept and barren rocky outcrop became our home. There was little of our natural hunting food source, so we ate rabbits and seabirds and the occasional hardy deer that crossed our path.

As wolves, we couldn't live on the surface; it was too dangerous, so we ventured underground in the sprawling subterranean caves.

There, the litter was born. The pack nurtured the wolf cubs to acclimatise to living underground – there was no moon to howl at. Wolves are an amazingly adaptable creature and these primeval instincts have allowed us to live in a whole range of habitats across the entire world.

We learned how to harvest the sea and ate fish. Fishing at high tide was a very enjoyable experience as the water came right inside the caves and brought the fruits of the sea with it.

Our eyesight and sense of smell became more acute. Our natural instincts to once again tread softly through the forest never diminished. However, we could not venture out on to the surface because of the danger and closeness of humans who constantly strived for our destruction and extinction. We want to live away from human interference but recognise the hatred that still exists, and wolves cannot step above ground.

When on one occasion an alpha wolf did embark on an investigation and, briefly, did one night go on to the surface to take stock of the situation, he was spotted, and following on from that, no further reckless misadventures were considered. The elder wolves took this young, inexperienced alpha male in hand to prevent further foolishness.

This incident happened in 1888 and was documented in the national media as a potential wolf sighting by a gamekeeper in Scotland. Fortunately, many dismissed this as a misidentification of a feral domesticated dog or trick of the moonlight.

So that is how it has been until now… something has changed on the surface and human activity has all but been silenced or come to a stop. The sound of humans has faded away to an almost unheard whisper. The wolves sense that man maybe is no longer a threat or has been weakened somehow.

How can this be? What has happened to the wolves' human persecutors? Have they gone away?

What the wolves also sense and smell is the return of the woodlands and forests that were once their kingdom. Trees have replaced the forests hacked down by humans centuries before, and new, mysterious thick forests complete with their unmistakable sounds that permeate the subterranean world of the wolves appear to be returning.

There is but one thing to do next. The boldest, bravest and most experienced wolf – the alpha and leader of the pack – must investigate and step out into the sunlight of their native Britain for the first time in centuries.

Going North

It was nine thirty in the morning, and Jack Green sat on the motorway in the rain. Not on the tarmac itself, of course – he had no desire to do that – but in his somewhat scuffed Ford Fiesta that might once have been a nice shade of silver. He was on the northbound carriageway of the M6, just past Keele Services, wishing he'd stopped to buy a cup of coffee.

It was mid-October 2022. After a traumatic two years fighting

Covid-19, the country had returned to something a-bit-like-normal-with-facemasks-sometimes, and he was, for the second time since July, taking an overdue holiday. His destination? A remote corner of north-west Scotland. The purpose? He was tracking wolves.

Jack smiled to himself every time he thought of this. It was what he'd told a work colleague the previous afternoon and had got the predictable response: "No, you don't need to go to Scotland. Go to Wolverhampton. That's where you'll find wolves!" They had both laughed, and Jack had to admit how odd, possibly silly, it sounded. He'd left it at that and talked about hillwalking and camping, which would also be part of the trip. Then, a member of the public came in to ask how to help a lame hedgehog – they worked at a wildlife rescue charity near Gloucester. After that, they were busy for the rest of the day tending to the animals currently in their care.

The traffic inched forward. The sky ahead looked determinedly grey and Jack wondered if this foretold the week to come. After a summer of mixed weather and several torrential downpours, he hoped not. A thin rain spattered the windscreen and gradually the traffic moved on, towards some unseen obstacle that blocked the road an unknown distance ahead. To his chagrin, the southbound traffic flowed smoothly. He had a long drive ahead and, even though he'd planned a stop at a campsite by Loch Lomond, if things didn't speed up, it was going to be a long day. Jack shifted his position in his seat, adjusted the radio, which made the reception irreversibly worse, and turned it off.

Slowly, after hours it seemed, but in fact about twenty minutes later, it looked as if the traffic was starting to move. One by one, cars, lorries and coaches began to speed up and spread out. At last things were moving again.

Wolves, Jack thought, and smiled again. How weird and wonderful would it be if the stories were true. Wolves actually living in Britain! Wild, in every sense! It was an established fact, however, that the last wolf in Britain was shot near Inverness in 1743. And yet the stories persisted. Mostly in tales and legend, it is true, but in the last couple of years, there had been rumours of sightings made by climbers and hillwalkers in the remotest and most rugged mountains of Scotland. On their own, none of these stories amounted to much, just rumour inflated by exaggeration. But, on a walking holiday in the summer of 2022, Jack had pricked up his ears when he had heard something similar, not from a fellow mountaineer, but from a shepherd he'd met below the mountain Slioch, near the village of Kinlochewe.

This story was different. The shepherd was a taciturn man in his fifties, and it was a bit of luck meeting him. Half an hour earlier, Jack had seen the carcass of a dead sheep wedged into a ravine. He'd noted where it was on his map and planned to find someone to tell later. Dead or not, the animal would still need accounting for. As it happened, the shepherd knew already and said it was from his flock. He thought it had been frightened into running over a short cliff. Normally, he'd said, this could have been a dog off the lead – an occasional happening in the tourist season – but the evidence didn't match.

"But these paw prints were big," said the shepherd, "and different to any dog I've ever seen, and from an animal with a long stride; they were a real distance apart."

"What could it have been?" prompted Jack.

"Well, we're a long way from the West Country, so it's not the Beast of Bodmin. And they *say* the last wolf was shot in the eighteenth century." He shrugged and left the idea hanging.

Jack was silent for a while. Then, with a twinge of embarrassment at his selfishness, decided to be practical.

"Is it safe to walk around here?"

The shepherd smiled a short sharp laugh, but not unkindly. "Oh yes. It's fine. Even if it is a wolf or wolves, they'll not harm you. We're the ultimate predator, remember. Only a really desperate animal will attack a human, unless they or their young are threatened first. If it's wolves, they'll know all about how dangerous *we* can be!"

***

Jack had read a little about wolves, but now he began in earnest. On his returning home, he had started digging around, trying to find out more about these beasts of legend. He scoured the internet for reference material. He read blogs written by outdoor types, in case they turned up anything of a pattern in alleged sightings; and indeed, there were a few, but they were all inconclusive and the threads always dried up after a couple of comments. He went to the local library and borrowed every book that might be relevant, and even arranged for books on inter-library loan. With this single-minded enthusiasm and his own slightly scrawny looks, it didn't take long before someone dubbed him "wolf man".

It was one of the library staff, a short, rotund man with close-cropped hair, in his late twenties – Jack's own age – who was often busy with publicity work for library events. He clearly thought he was the local wit. Calling in one Saturday morning to collect a book, Jack was greeted with a laugh and "Hello, wolf man!". Jack laughed it off, but even though it did not seem to be intended unkindly, it made him feel uneasy. Too familiar with the wrong end of name-calling at school, he never made fun of others unless they were good friends and the joke would be understood. The teasing happened a few more times and Jack noticed some of the librarian's colleagues begin to copy him. On what seemed like the twentieth occasion, Jack turned round, heart beating, and said: "That's not my name. Please stop saying that."

He'd caught the others off guard and the librarian's reply was sarcastically defensive. "Oh! Sorry!" Then he thought better of it. "Ah, sorry… that sounded bad. I just thought, you know, all this reading about wolves, it's like you're a famous naturalist studying wolves and nothing else, so you're, you know, *the wolf man*." He raised his fingers in the air to indicate inverted commas.

Jack was momentarily flummoxed. He hadn't known what to expect, but it wasn't this. "Well, OK, but it's not right. I've got a name. It is Jack or Mr Green for that matter, which you can see on the screen every time I borrow a book. Same as you've got a name (Jack looked at the librarian's ID tag)… Steven. Please, just use my name. That would be much… easier."

"OK," replied Steven. He seemed chastened and a bit embarrassed. "Sorry. Here's your latest volume of *Yellowstone Wolves in the Wild*. It looks really good, actually. I might read it myself when you're done."

Jack took the book and nodded his thanks. He turned to go. Steven spoke again. "Just in case you *are* a famous naturalist, and even if you're not, well, I'm sorry. I didn't mean to be rude, and good luck with what you're working on."

Jack smiled. "Well, I am a naturalist in a way. But I'm not famous. I'll let you know how I get on."

***

The episode at the library had made Jack think of his school days. To say he'd had either a happy or an unhappy childhood was too simple. Like lots of people, he imagined, it was both, sometimes simultaneously. His parents had not been rich and he and his brother had a modest upbringing in the village of Long Lydbrook on the western edges of the Forest of Dean. It was a loving family, not perfect, but caring. His hard-working parents and generally indulgent grandparents usually found a way to make time for Jack and his older brother, Chris, even if only to read a story in the evening.

His mother's dad – Grandad Pete – was always Jack's favourite. In his younger days he'd been a miner in the forest and had a seemingly endless collection of stories about adventures underground and in the deep woods, all told with a smattering of the old forest dialect. Grandad Pete, with an old injury from the mines and only a part-time job, would sometimes help the boys with homework and read to them later. One of the boys' favourites was *The Minpins* by Roald Dahl. To Chris and Jack, the Forest of Sin was always the real Forest of Dean and the mysteries of the real and imagined forests seemed to merge with one another. No matter how many times he heard the story, and then later when he read it himself, Jack was mesmerised by the language, the beautiful illustrations, and the possibility that there really was an undiscovered world out there if only he knew where to look.

One of their favourite games was to play twenty questions with the different characters. Whichever one they started with, it usually ended up with the Terrible Blood-suckling Tooth-pluckling Stone-chuckling Spittler or, even worse, the fearsome Red-Hot Smoke-Belching Gruncher. They could never decide if these two monsters were one and the same, but the talk always came round to what the Spittler-cum-Gruncher might actually be.

"It's a dragon escaped from Wales," insisted Chris. "I bet it is!"

Jack disagreed. "Can't be a dragon. It doesn't fly. It's a ginormous dog or something, with two heads."

"Or maybe it's a wolf, like the ones who used to roam these lands," suggested Grandad Pete. "People are always scared of wolves, and I bet their breath would really steam when the air is cold."

These memories, like indelible video images, stayed with Jack, fresh and clear and with fondness. It was not the same with his memories of school, though. It hadn't been all bad, of course, and he'd done well with schoolwork, progressing eventually to sixth form college to study science A levels. There, it was biology that opened up the natural world that became his real fascination. University had been a distinct possibility, but his dad's illness and the strain this put on his mum had led him to opt instead for a job locally. It just seemed right that he could stay at or near home and help from time to time.

Before that, though, halfway through primary school, a couple of other boys had noticed that Jack's clothes were always a bit scruffy and never new. This was true, and even at this age Jack hated having always to wear Chris' hand-me-down school uniform. Why, in reality, this should surprise people, thought Jack, he didn't really know. Lots of other children seemed to be in the same boat. But the bullies had decided to bait Jack anyway. They made his life a misery, taunting him and laughing: "Too poor to get your own clothes, hey, Jack?" and "Jack Green the Grunge Boy.". They'd get others to taunt and laugh, and always did this out of sight of adults. It wasn't every day, but just enough to make Jack anxious most of the time. Jack had a couple of good friends – also younger brothers who wore hand-me-down clothes – but that wasn't enough protection and they caught the wrath of the bullies too. Jack tried to keep his head down and do his best with his work. He knew his dad was unwell and his mum had plenty to worry about, so he kept the two worlds separate as far as he could.

One of the bullies Jack could remember well. Martin Grough. Taller than Jack and even then very strong, Martin was, in truth, of a similar background. But he always made out he was better than the others, and it always seemed to the children that the teachers believed him. He was the star of the football team, always had the lead in the school play and had the knack of being able to say the right thing to the right people just when he needed to. He was boastful and arrogant, and a charmer when he wanted something. He didn't seem to care that so many of his peers disliked him for it. And why indeed should he? His chosen way of dealing with the world seemed to work, after all, and there was no one to put him in his place.

To Jack's dismay, things continued much the same at secondary school. There was the saving grace, if it could be called that, that there were plenty of others for Martin to torment, but he often came back to Jack and took pleasure from the persecution. Cleverly, he and his henchmen never went as far as a full beating up, so, in a school which seemed to favour the survival of the fittest, it was really difficult to find a convincing way to complain. Jack read voraciously and focused on his studies instead. It paid off and he began to develop a more mature understanding of the natural world, especially of wild animals under threat of extinction. Encouraged by a friend, he also joined the local scouts and discovered a love of the outdoors for its own sake, which fitted neatly with his passion for wildlife.

Martin, Jack knew, was now a successful TV chat show host. Having reached prime time TV when still so young, he was something of a celebrity in his own right. He was, apparently, already immensely wealthy, but he was more famous, infamous really, for his interview style: charming and friendly but always with a malicious question as a sting in the tail. Film stars and pop musicians queued up to get on his show because of the ratings, but they must all have dreaded that final question. Once a bully, it seemed, always a bully.

For Jack, on the other hand, sixth form college without Martin had been a liberation. He made friends, plunged into his studies and excelled at exams. Having decided against university, he found his first job at a vet's, and then a longer-term prospect at a wildlife rescue centre. This wasn't the one he worked at now, but at the time it had promised a lot and seemed like a good idea.

***

Jack was nudged back to the present moment. An amber fuel warning light on the dashboard announced that he could drive for another fifty miles on the remaining fuel.

Feeling silly, Jack remembered he had forgotten to fill up with petrol early that morning. Then he felt embarrassed at his own embarrassment; fifty miles was a long way and there would be plenty of service stations before he ran out of fuel. Relaxing back into the driving, he began to look out for signposts announcing "Services".

Awakenings

Far away – yet getting ever closer – in the Scottish Highlands, the alpha wolf sat completely still at the entrance to the cave, transfixed like a mysterious stone sentinel painted by moonlight. Simply staring at the landscape, the alpha and members of the wolf pack had made a few sorties above ground but taking extra care not to communicate and howl and alert humans to their presence. But the human activity had been very quiet for a long period of time now. The omega wolf silently emerged from the mouth of the cave and both wolves sat side by side, gazing out across the lunar world with an increasing sense of excitement. What they could keenly sense and smell was the very breath of the forest. Their true home.

Ducks in a Row

Sustained by a quick cup of coffee and a full tank of petrol, Jack continued north along the M6. Across the long sweeping bridge over the Manchester Ship Canal, past signposts to Warrington, Wigan and Leyland, on he drove.

Around Preston, past Lancaster and towards the Lake District. A signpost to Kendal. Then the twists and turns as the road followed a steep-sided valley. Here, it cut between the eastern edge of the Lakes and where, marking the transition to the Pennines, the Howgill Fells loomed ominously in a luminescent grey light. The high hills were covered alternately with heather and, despite the season, patches of startlingly green grass.

After that, a slight dip past the long village of Tebay, before another ascent, this time over Shap Summit, the motorway's highest point. Beyond that, past Penrith and Carlisle and, just over the River Eden, the border with Scotland at Gretna.

As he drove, Jack attempted to get his ideas in order. For he wasn't just going camping and hoping to see a wolf. In Scotland, he'd be meeting a talented wildlife photographer and together they'd be attempting not only to find, but to document in pictures the wolves they hoped to track. The photographer, Sian Jones, was a stickler for detail and Jack knew he had to have facts at his fingertips and a reason for choosing the most likely place to find their "prey".

Wolves, Jack knew, were so much part of legend and folklore that at first it was difficult to unpick fact from fantasy. First, he had put aside all the tales of werewolves, fairy tales and horror stories and tried to find out the basics. The formal Latin name was a good start: *Canis lupus*. This established the very clear link with the dog family, of which the wolf is the largest member. As the largest wild dog, an adult grey wolf can be anything from four to six feet long, and with legs extended while running, it will look considerably longer. It has large feet, a straight tail and a long snout. Its head is broader than most other species of dog, which, with its very noticeable teeth, adds to the general sense of ferocity. The forward-facing eyes of a predator rounded off the picture nicely. In profile, the grey wolf, especially those not yet fully mature, looked suspiciously like the Alsatian dogs favoured by the police. Jack found it fascinating that this wild animal – so very wild and ferocious according to legend – was the origin of the domestic dog, "man's best friend".

Wolves, he discovered, were very sociable animals, and he supposed this was a prerequisite for living successfully in a pack. Each of these was a large extended family, supporting the dominant male and the female, who would be the parents of most of the pack. These would be the breeding pair but the efforts of the pack would go to supporting more than the new litter. Older wolves would educate the younger ones, and the middle-ranking animals would create the heart of a formidable hunting team. Some research showed that older and injured wolves were helped by the rest of the group, so there was no doubt that each pack was a complex social unit. There were strict hierarchies, but also a considerable degree of cooperation which worked to protect and strengthen the family as a whole.

Mostly, packs were extended families with the main breeding pair naturally at the centre, or more accurately, the apex. Sometimes, and this seemed to fit with artificially created packs of "rescued" wolves returned into the wild, there would be a dominant alpha male and corresponding female. The same "family" structure would follow, but the alpha positions tended to be based much more on physical dominance than lineage. Logically enough, these packs could be more volatile.

Contemplating family dynamics, Jack had looked up the meaning of "lone wolf". He knew its metaphorical meaning but he was curious about its origins. As social pack animals, it was relatively rare for wolves to reject individuals. So, while lone wolves *might* be those who unsuccessfully challenged the alpha and were excluded from the pack, it would be just as likely that a lone animal would be one who had reached breeding age but could not breed in its own pack. Naturally, it would leave and search elsewhere for a mate.

This got Jack thinking. If he had pieced together the evidence correctly and he and Sian did track the wolves he believed were there, that would only be one pack. And, unless the shape of the wolf family unit had changed over the last three hundred years, it would be extraordinary if just the one pack existed. Logically, there ought to be two or three, or more. This, he hoped, significantly increased their chances of finding at least one of them.

Wolves were carnivores, and as their prey, they favoured large ruminants – hoofed, grazing animals – so in Europe this would have meant deer, and in the days when wolves were numerous, also cattle. However, animals such as sheep, although theoretically a target (Jack thought back to his meeting with the shepherd a couple of months earlier) would not be their first choice of prey. If an adult wolf could eat eight to nine kilograms of meat in a meal, and each hunt would ideally satisfy the whole pack, a large animal would definitely be preferable. And this made sense. In the spine-chilling tales from cold winters in Russia, there was often a horse-drawn sleigh chased by a pack of hungry wolves. A terrifying experience, no doubt, but the cool-headed human would know that it was primarily the horse that the wolves were after, not the thin-fleshed human occupants of the sleigh. Still, Jack supposed, while he wasn't about to volunteer to put that theory to the test, he could see how the wolves had acquired their fearsome reputation, at least partly for the wrong reasons.

***

The place of the wolf in history was also something that Jack found fascinating. The last wolf in Britain was killed sometime in the mid-eighteenth century – different accounts made different claims, some as late as the 1760s – but it was clear that, even by that time, they were all but extinct after centuries of persecution.

Wolves featured in many ancient tales that were woven into the fabric of history where legend blended with reality. Romulus and Remus, traditionally the founders of Rome, were supposed to have been suckled by a she-wolf as infants. Wolves made other appearances in myth and legend, prominently in Norse culture and also with the Inuit, Egyptians and Turks.

The harsh reality, however, was that wolves ate the animals that humans wanted for themselves, or perhaps it was the other way round. The moment human population growth put pressure on the ecosystems that had supported wolves for millennia, there was tension. Wolves may have been the creatures of myth and legend, but more importantly they lived in ancient forests upon which the humans encroached more and more.

In the time of the Romans, wolves were plentiful in Britain, and they remained so through the Dark Ages and beyond. Medieval kings frequently called for forests to be cleared and wolves to be killed. Debts or taxes were converted to wolf skins. Wolves were fair game nearly all-year round, and for the most part, they were trapped rather than hunted. But in January, wolf hunting was the prerogative of the rich landowners and nobles. It was also the month when wolves were most visible in the forests and the time when, pressed hard by cold weather, they would venture closer to villages and farms to prey on easy-to-catch domestic animals.

In Wales, it is thought that the last wolf was killed in 1166, at least partly as a result of the ruthless colonisation of Wales by the Norman kings of England. In 1281, King Edward I ordered the extermination of all wolves in England, and it seems that the last wolf in the country was killed, possibly in Kent, at some time in the reign of Henry VII, the first Tudor monarch. In Scotland, it was a different story. Wolves remained endemic and were perceived as a real threat to travellers. In the sixteenth and seventeenth centuries, there was an increase in the building of roadside shelters for travellers – "spitals" as they were called – not just as protection against the weather but also specifically against wolves. Although wolves probably disappeared from lowland Scotland fairly early in this period, the wolves of the Highlands, still with vast forests to inhabit, lived on for a long time.

While Jack knew that the last recorded wolf in Scotland was supposed to have been killed in 1743, it was by no means clear that this meant all wolves had gone from the Highlands. It was this thin thread that had captured Jack's imagination and set him off "hunting" for wolves himself.

***

After his meeting with the shepherd of Kinlochewe, Jack had become convinced that it was something worth investigating. While references to sightings online were only occasional and generally poorly substantiated, Jack did begin to see a pattern. All the references were to activity north of the Great Glen, and most were from an area north of the A832 which runs east-west from Black Isle to Gairloch. He decided to start looking for himself.

So, in mid-september 2022, with lockdown restrictions mostly lifted, he headed north for ten days' holiday. His goal had been Torridon, and in particular the land beyond the towering peaks of Liathach and Beinn Eighe, the Flowerdale Forest. No longer a forest as the word is understood today, this was a remote area of rough, steep-sided mountains, heath and bog, a treacherous area for the unwary. He'd spent a couple of nights in Torridon Youth Hostel, where he'd left his car, and then set off, a little apprehensively, with backpack, provisions and a small tent.

The first part of his journey was straightforward. For six kilometres or so, he followed the well-trodden path which led rock climbers to the monumental Triple Buttress of Coinneach Mhor, one of the western peaks of Beinn Eighe. This was not his destination, however. The path wound its way gradually higher around the shoulder of the mountain, and just before the buttresses came into view, he took a different direction. Heading due north, he began a gradual descent on to lower ground, an area which would be wet underfoot and littered with lochans and a multitude of streams and areas of bog. From this no man's land sprang a stream that quickly became a river flowing north-east – the Grudie. To the left of that, if you were facing downstream, sat the steep-sided, flat-topped mountain of Beinn a' Chearcaill. This was his destination. From there, if the weather held, he'd get clear views in all directions.

It was a hard scramble to the plateau, on a muggy overcast day, with only a hint of breeze to keep the infamous midges of the Highlands at bay. He took a semicircular route on the south-eastern flank to avoid the steepest slopes, so it was late afternoon before he stopped at a small lochan hundred metres below and a kilometre east of the summit: a perfect spot to camp. And although quite exposed at this height, it was a beautiful place. He was glad to pitch his tent, cook and eat. Refreshed from his meal he ascended the gentle slope to the nearby "top", as he'd heard subsidiary summits called.

The evening was still and the grey half-light of the long northern evening rendered the scenery deceptively flat. Cloud cover was more or less complete but, with the cloud base well above the mountains, the views were extensive. He felt as if he was in an entirely different world to the one, he'd left at the youth hostel, just a few kilometres away. Apart from the occasional bird call, he was enveloped in a tangible silence.

Sitting on a smooth rock on this peak, he faced north and watched the evening colours change imperceptibly. He wondered just how realistic his search was going to be.

The following morning, Jack left his tent pitched. He had the food and the time to stay another night if need be and if weather permitted, so with just his lunch, water, camera and binoculars to hand, he climbed the remaining distance to the summit. The sky had changed. Gone was the flat grey sky. Now there was a fresher breeze, patches of blue and regiments of white cumulus clouds sailing across the sky. The air was bright and clear. His spirits rose. He marvelled at how the summit area was almost perfectly flat; great slabs of sandstone were a tabletop upon which were scattered stones of varying size, like breakfast crumbs left by a giant. Standing at the summit he scanned the surrounding country, first with the naked eye, then with binoculars.

In truth, he didn't know what to expect and, in reality, he didn't really know what he was looking for. At this height, he was unlikely to spot much moving. True, he would see anyone walking or climbing so long as their clothing was brightly coloured, but beyond that, would he see a wolf? Their colouring, he knew, wasn't automatically grey, so even wolves from the same litter could have colours varying from nearly black through to a grey tinted with amber and the gold of straw. In this mottled landscape, any of those colours would be a perfect disguise. At this distance, with his inexpensive binoculars, what chance did he have of seeing an animal so perfectly camouflaged?

He decided not to worry about the apparent fruitlessness of his expedition. Instead, he would enjoy the day. Leaning against a boulder, he took to slowly sweeping the valleys below with binoculars.

For a couple of hours, occasionally changing his direction of view, there was nothing out of the ordinary. Then, on a large area of flat bare rock in the valley bottom to the north-west, something white. Without the glasses, just a distant bright spot. Through binoculars, however, it was something altogether different. The remains of a red deer, the skeleton mostly stripped of flesh and the bones bleached by the sun. Not recent, then, but unusually sited. Why was it on the rock, almost as if the barren platform had been a place of last resort? He'd seen deer carcasses before, but, usually, it was where the animal had got trapped in an area of bog and, unable to escape, had eventually collapsed from exhaustion and hunger. This location struck him as odd. Could this have been the end of a chase? Is this where the hunted had finally turned to face the hunters?

The rest of the day he saw nothing else of note and he doubted whether he'd really expected to. The deer carcass had been unusual but it was not conclusive. And while this area was remote, it wasn't *that* remote. *He'd* got here fairly easy, after all. Perhaps he should look elsewhere.

The following evening, he was back at Torridon Youth Hostel, showered and refreshed and exchanging stories with other walkers and climbers. Afraid of being laughed at, he didn't declare his interest in wolves, but chatting to a few of the others, he did describe the deer skeleton. "Odd" and "Could be anything" seemed to be verdicts, but one young Scotsman pricked his ears up and said:

"You never know, we might have a big cat up here after all…" He paused for dramatic effect. "There've been several deer killed over towards An Teallach that the locals can't account for. Not shot or ill. Just killed. Throats torn out so far as anyone can tell, and then the meat mostly stripped from the bone." He laughed. "Must be one big cat!"

**

Later, Jack got out his maps. An Teallach was a formidable looking double-peaked mountain about thirty miles north-east as the crow flies, and sixty miles by road. It might be worth investigating. One last throw of the dice before setting off back home via the Lake District, where he'd arranged to meet up with friends. And this time he might stick to the valleys. Not out of fear for a big cat, but because he might learn more from listening to the stories of others who knew the area better.

By lunchtime the next day, he had stopped in the car park of the Dundonnell Hotel, not far from the shores of Little Loch Broom. Behind the hotel were the northern outlying slopes of An Teallach and, in front, a small salt marsh at the head of the loch. The weather had changed, and now heavy drops of rain fell in short and ferociously drenching showers. He loved to walk in the mountains, and while he knew he couldn't do that without being rained on occasionally, he was still glad of an excuse not to be on the hills.

Walking into the public bar, he stopped a moment to let his eyes adjust to the dimmer light. It was a large room, almost cavernous. At the far end, a country and western band was rehearsing, perhaps for an evening gig. Apart from the barman and a small handful of people at distant tables, the bar was empty. He approached the bar and asked if food was available. The barman nodded and pointed to some laminated menus.

"What will you drink?" The barman spoke with a Glaswegian accent, but in a quiet and measured way, so it wasn't too difficult to follow.

"Oh, just a pint of orange juice and lemonade, please." Jack inspected the menu. "And a ham and cheese toastie to go with it."

"No problem."

The barman placed the drink in front of Jack, then scribbled the order on a notepad, tore it off with a flourish and walked round a corner to take it to the kitchen. On the wall behind the bar, in a gap between rows of bottles, was a framed print. It showed what might have been a medieval scene, although it had a look of Victorian romance about it. Ferocious hunting dogs, like angry hairy greyhounds, surrounded a wounded and snarling wolf twice their size. Various kilted highlanders were joining the kill. One of them, especially fierce with a plaited beard and a coat of animal skin, stood with his arm aloft, a spear poised to strike and his face in a grimace. Frozen in the moment, it was difficult to decide which animal was the wildest: wolf, dog or man? And who, Jack wondered, was most fearful?

The barman returned with Jack's sandwich, obviously just toasted, with melted cheese still running out of one corner.

Jack took the plate and sat on a bar stool. "Thanks." He gestured at the print. "Not many of those left," he said, leaving his enquiry as open as possible.

"Well, not many deerhounds around, that's true. And the rest is all Victorian fancy dress. I doubt many real highlanders would have worn skins like that."

Jack nodded and waited. He looked back at the print.

"As for the wolves," the barman continued, "well, that's a funny thing. They're all gone, of course, centuries ago. Although there is talk of bringing them back, further west. The landowner of the Alladale Estate wants to rewild. Not a bad idea, if you ask me. They'd keep the deer down and that would let some of the forest regrow. And apparently there's a wolf rescue centre in Shropshire or Wales or somewhere; you know – they take in wolves who've been in zoos. They could send some up here."

"Could they survive? Here?" asked Jack.

"Maybe," was the reply. "And something *has* been killing deer over the last few months. Quite cleanly, so they say, but not humans. Some kind of big dog is on the loose, I reckon. It's been having a great time during lockdown." The barman laughed. "And not just big. Pretty fierce too." He wiped the already gleaming and spotless bar. "Let me know if you need anything else."

Pathways

The wolf ran quickly through the thick undergrowth and into the mouth of the cave, travelling fast, down to the safety of the den. It had sensed the presence of humans and had smelled that unmistakable smell of danger. However, this was not from human but from another source. The observed humans had not given a natural fear but something else. There seemed to be a threat but from something in a different realm.

Good Times and Bad Times

By the time Jack had reached the campsite by Loch Lomond, day was becoming evening with a definite twist of autumn. There was a noticeable coolness to the air. Thin cloud was breaking up to reveal an open sky and the first pinpoint stars were flickering into life. The moon, midway between its first quarter and a full disc, was already bright and clear. At "ground" level, lights across the water were reflected in the loch.

As dusk gathered, Jack lost no time in checking in with the camp warden and pitching his tent. Adding an extra layer of clothes, he put his sleeping mat on the grass in front of the tent, made himself comfortable and cooked some pasta on his small camping stove.

Before long, the light of the evening was gone. Further to his right along the shore was a hotel, and beyond that, the lochside village of Luss. The water of the loch itself was calm and inky dark. "Floating" in front of him, and slightly to the right, was the wood-covered isle of Inchlonaig. With only a few others at the campsite, there was little noise, only really a low murmuring and the clink of cutlery and cooking pots. He inspected his food with his head torch. Dazzled by the reflection of the beam in the steel bowl, he switched it off. Not a problem, he thought; he could eat by the light of the moon and then he'd see something other than the inside of the mess tin. He turned the stove off too, and watched the flames putter-putter-putter, shrinking to a memory of blue.

The night was still and, despite the uncertainty of his quest, Jack felt happy.

He thought about the word. Was it quite the right one? He was never sure and, every time he heard someone say they were happy, he wondered what they meant, exactly. For himself, he wasn't sure happiness was the best description. This was not to say he was in any way miserable, far from it. But life seemed too complicated for the fairy tale idea of happiness to fit properly.

Looking out over the water, he tried to get a sense of what these thoughts meant. For this moment, "content" was probably a better word. He enjoyed his current job, where everything seemed to work smoothly, even when they were busy. The manager, who described a well-organised workplace as a healthy ecosystem, was about to retire. She was actively encouraging Jack to apply for the position, so things were definitely on the up. But other memories crept in – school and his dad's illness – so that "happy" just seemed a bit simplistic.

At home, he *had* been happy in the sense that his was a loving family, but that had been, and still was, coloured by his father's multiple sclerosis, which had appeared when Jack was in his early teens. This cruel disease had started with mild difficulties with movement and balance; now his dad was mostly bed-ridden and needed assistance with tasks that most people take for granted. Jack and his brother helped their mum as much as they could, and the council had helped pay for carers, but it was still hard – far harder than their mum would let on. But she, and in fact their dad too, kept insisting the boys should lead their own lives. Chris, now married, and Jack could see the continual challenges that their parents faced, so it was difficult to get the balance right.

And then there had been Jack's previous job, in almost every respect, a disaster. It had started well. He had been an assistant at a local animal and wildlife welfare charity, helping to look after rescued stray cats and dogs and, increasingly, injured or half-starved wild animals brought in by members of the public. There were hedgehogs, foxes of all ages and squirrels, once a badger, and, in fact, most small mammals as well as larger ones such as muntjac deer, and even once an adult roe deer. It was the foxes that fascinated Jack, though. Half-wolf, half-dog, where did they fit in on the spectrum between "savage beast" and "man's best friend"?

One of several branches of a larger organisation, the rescue centre was a busy place, with four full-time staff including the manager, Paul, plus a couple of part-time colleagues who did weekends. A local vet visited on a regular basis and Jack listened carefully to everything she explained. Jack himself seemed a natural and the job title of assistant didn't really do justice to his role. He was good with the animals and his knowledge of biology and chemistry was a real help. Plus, Jack's careful research skills and growing knowledge meant his colleagues would often ask him first for his ideas before going to see the manager.

That had been the start of it, really. Jack had never put himself forward as any kind of expert, but his good memory and easy manner seemed to mean that others came to ask his advice anyway. Paul took this badly. Very, very badly.

In the few months it had taken Jack to settle properly into the job, Paul had taken a dislike to him and, gradually, this changed to actively putting him down, then to what could only be described as persecution. There were plenty of cruel jibes, especially about Jack's dad, and he never missed an opportunity to take issue with the tiniest thing he saw Jack doing or saying. Paul criticised the way Jack did things, even though Jack – and his co-workers – could see nothing wrong in the things Paul picked on.

In reality, there was nothing that Paul should have complained about. Jack knew that in terms of the work he was doing, he always followed the correct procedures, and he never said or did anything "above his station" as an assistant. He certainly never assumed knowledge he didn't have, and once he realised Paul's back was up, he tried to discourage the others from asking his advice. Paul couldn't fault Jack's work, but he did so anyway and the persecution continued.

Jack hoped it would go away. He hoped that if he showed he was good at the job and was content to do what his job description said, things would be all right. But Paul's persecution did not go away. If anything, it got worse. Frequently, he tried to catch Jack out, often asking him difficult questions beyond the scope of his responsibilities. When Jack was right, Paul would make some sneering comment about Jack being "overeducated". When Jack couldn't give an immediate answer, Paul would mock him: "So, not so book-smart now are we?"

And yet Jack knew he was doing a good job. He was good – very good – with the animals (the vet had said so more than once), he was helpful to the public, and any paperwork required was always done properly. When solutions to problems weren't obvious, he used his initiative, found an answer or asked for advice – even though this meant going to Paul to ask for "help". And still, in Paul's eyes, Jack could never get it right.

Jack was miserable and he could see no end to this torture in sight. Chris, his brother, had already urged him to leave, but Jack was hesitant. It was at least a job, and he couldn't afford not to have one, nor the uncertainty of trying to find one. And he was scared that Paul would never write him a good reference. He was trapped.

Then one evening, in conversation with Sandra, an old friend from college, it dawned on Jack that Paul saw him as some kind of threat. This became more obvious when Jack began to pick up stories about Paul's own track record. He had, it seemed, a reputation for making mistakes, lying to cover them up, for being rude to the public, and even for being cruel to the animals in his care. The realisation was horrifying. If Paul really did feel threatened, like a wild animal cornered, there might be no limits to what he would do.

After nearly two years of this, and not for the first time thinking of how ineffective his schools had been at dealing with bullies, Jack decided to make a formal complaint. He found the right policies and checked to see whom he should speak to first. His heart sank. Paul was his line manager, and it was Paul to whom he would have to complain – about Paul!

After a telephone call to head office, this really did turn out to be what Jack had to do.

"The first thing you'll need to do is address the issue with the person you think is causing the problem. Without doing that, no complaint will be valid."

Jack tried to explain but did not get a sympathetic response. It seemed as if the HR department was much more concerned about keeping the charity out of trouble than it was with helping its employees. Clearly, they thought much more about "Resources" than they did about "Human".

So, he resolved to speak to Paul anyway. He knew that he should be allowed to have a witness to the conversation, but he didn't want any of his colleagues to get on the wrong side of Paul. Nor was he a member of a trade union, who might have lent support, so Jack resigned himself to doing it alone. He knew this would be a difficult experience. But who knew? Maybe Paul would be surprised into mending his ways.

Jack fixed an appointment with Paul. When the time came, it was a meeting in the manager's small office, overflowing with piles of paper and out-of-date reference books. They sat either side of the desk, and for Jack, uncomfortably close to each other. Paul seemed to relish Jack's discomfort. Acting much more calmly than he felt inside, Jack explained that he thought Paul was picking on him unfairly, and that he felt that for some reason Paul disliked him. In turn, he said, this was influencing Paul's view of Jack's work and leading to unfair criticism.

Paul, a thin, sallow-faced man in his mid-fifties, started by shrugging it off.

"No, I don't know what you mean. If I've criticised you, it's because you've fallen down on the job."

Jack, hands sweating and more breathless than he would have wished, gave some examples. He said he had a record of the various incidents going back about six months and that in fact none of them had shown his work as defective.

Paul, like many cunning bullies, played it down and avoided that point. "You're imagining things. I just expect high standards. I don't mollycoddle anyone and I'm not about to start now." He looked at Jack, challenging him to take it further. Jack, to his own surprise, made one more attempt.

"I'd just like to be treated like everyone else. You don't speak to the others in the way you speak to me. I'd like it to stop, please."

Paul looked at Jack for a long moment. "I don't have a problem with you, Jack. But it looks like you've got one with me. Get over it and go to work." And then, as Jack rose to leave the office, he spoke quietly, "Don't try this again."

Jack couldn't believe his ears. "Is that a threat?"

Paul spoke without looking up. "You're wasting time. Haven't you got animals to care for?"

***

For several weeks after the meeting, Paul seemed to be avoiding Jack, who began to think that maybe things really were getting better. No such luck. Rather than a change of heart by Paul, it was very much a false dawn.

One particularly busy Saturday, Paul called Jack in to help a member of the public with an injured fox. A grey-haired woman had seen it get hit by a moped outside her house. The RSPCA had been called but wouldn't be able to help for several hours, so she'd brought it to the rescue centre. Jack's job was to take the animal to a holding pen and, so far as possible, make it comfortable, awaiting the arrival of the vet in the evening. The fox, in an old cat-carrying box, was clearly in distress. Instead of leaving things to Jack, Paul took the box himself, pulling it clumsily from the woman and swinging it, actually swinging it, towards Jack. Inside the box, the fox shifted position, Paul lost his grip and the box fell to the floor.

There was a split second's silence. The woman stood open-mouthed. Jack immediately stooped to pick it up, first looking carefully inside to check which way the fox was lying. But before he could do anything else, Paul was shouting abuse, calling him all sorts of names and accusing Jack of being stupid and causing the accident.

Then there was another voice, a sharp "Stop!" It was the grey-haired woman. She turned to Paul, and in a quiet and determined voice spoke again.

"Stop it at once. It's not this young man's fault at all. I saw what happened. I've a good mind to report you!" Turning to Jack, she continued: "I'm sure *you* are doing brilliantly. Thank you for helping." Facing Paul again, she gave him a look. "And I'll be back to check on what you've done with that poor fox."

***

What Jack thought might at last be the end to the persecution by Paul turned out to be the complete opposite. The next week and the weeks after were worse than ever. Every evening, Jack would return to his flat exhausted, not from the work, but emotionally drained. He felt helpless and humiliated. Further calls to the charity's head office did nothing to help. Either he had to forget all about it or make a formal complaint, but the hidden message seemed to be warning him off, warning him to be "sensible" if he wanted a quiet life. And with plenty of other things to worry about, that is exactly what he did want.

Jack knew it was wrong to let Paul get away with it, but he felt at a loss as to what to do. He started job hunting online again, but nothing in the same line of work came up within the area. Weeks passed. Then, one evening, his phone blinked into life – there was an alert from an employment agency for just the job he was looking for. It could have been his current job, but twenty miles away and well out of the way of Paul. He took the plunge. Carefully, very carefully, he started filling out the on-screen application.

***

From behind Jack, car headlights swept across the campsite grass, illuminating the shoreline and very briefly, as the car turned, sending their beams sliding across the now still waters of Loch Lomond. Jack stirred from his thoughts and made a final scrape of his cooking pot-cum-bowl. Smiling to himself, he found the other pot, the one he always kept clean for boiling water, and relit the stove. A cup of tea would be just the ticket. What could be nicer than a warm brew on such a perfect evening?

Ahead lay a real adventure. Wolves! This time, Jack was sure that he'd narrowed down the right locations. If there were wolves out there, he was sure that he and Sian would find traces at least. And to see real wolves in Scotland? It really wasn't a dream. It really could be possible!

The water boiled. Jack dropped a teabag into his mug and found the handle to lift the pot. The water hissed and steamed as he poured. He squeezed and extracted the tea bag, enjoying the ritual. He added a splash of milk. Cradling the mug in both hands, he looked out across the loch.

The star-sprinkled sky was reflected in the water. The myriad sparks of light seemed to represent countless opportunities. And tomorrow and in the days to come, he just needed one opportunity to work out well. Jack smiled. Yes, "content". That seemed OK.

Secret Watcher

The wolf was watching everything whilst hiding in the dense undergrowth surrounding the campsite. The wolf's shadow fell against the edge of the campsite. However, the humans had not seen, heard or smelled the wolf's presence, their senses far inferior to the heightened senses of the wolf. The wolf was watching carefully and silently, then just as silently, the wolf disappeared back into the thick undergrowth.

The Call of the Wild

The next morning, Jack was up a little before the sun. He had a long day ahead of him and he wanted to be on the road without delay. But he also wanted to give himself the time to enjoy the day and the location.

In front of his tent, the waters of the loch were still. The air was cool, but the water had retained some of its heat from warmer weather. Atop the surface was a thin and patchy layer of mist, perhaps a couple of feet deep. It hugged the shoreline, and the islands further out seemed to be afloat in a sea of cloud.

Jack half expected to see an arm emerge from the water holding a magical sword, although what he really hoped to see in real life was one of the sea eagles that were nesting near the loch. Earlier in the year, two large white-tailed eagles had been seen spying out places to nest nearby. With a wingspan of up to two-and-a-half metres, they were large birds and would need a big tree. And the shores of Loch Lomond were ideal. Extensive areas of old, established woodland came down to the water's edge and there were many potentially good nesting sites. There were fish in the loch and, for a bird of their size, the sea itself was a few easy miles' flight away if they wanted a change of diet.

There had been a brief flurry of media activity on their arrival in the spring. These birds had not been seen near the loch for a long time – some said a century – but birds of prey in Scotland were gradually becoming better re-established. It looked as if this pair had taken advantage of the relative quiet brought about by the pandemic lockdown. The concern now was how they would adapt to the more "naturally" busy human activity as the country got back to normal. The RSPB and the National Park Authority had set up a protective exclusion zone around the nest site, and it seemed to have been agreed that the less publicity there was, the better.

There were, of course, a few voices of dissent, mainly from the farming community. Although sea eagles typically ate fish and smaller seabirds, even geese, they scavenged what they could find and were quite partial to rabbit and hare. There was a fear locally that they might target lambs and even sheep. However, when Jack had last looked for news on this, there seemed to be no reports of livestock lost. Nevertheless, Jack wondered, if eagles (albeit pretty big ones) caused this level of concern, what would farmers make of wolves, or even the idea of them?

***

If the birds were aloft, they should be quite easy to spot. So Jack, wondering if the mist would put them off, kept one eye on the sky. And while keeping "an eagle eye out" he set some water to boil. He made tea and some porridge and set about packing his gear and striking his tent. By eight fifteen, he was ready. Back in the car, he drove slowly out of the campsite and joined the main road. It was a real pleasure to follow the loch side and then continue north towards Crianlarich, Tyndrum and Glencoe, before going on to Fort William and the Great Glen.

The forecast was for generally dry weather for the next week or so, and the day promised to be clear and sunny. Following his route north would take him through some of the most striking scenery in the country, and it was a drive he would enjoy. However, he had more than beautiful views to think about. In particular, he was trying to put his "wolf hunt" into some kind of context that made sense.

Initially, it was all about his curiosity. Of course, he was fascinated with wildlife and his experience of foxes had left him more and more inquisitive about the different species of wild dog. But as his reading had widened, he began to see how the possibility of wolves in Britain fitted right in with the growing movement to "rewild". This, he discovered, was exactly what it sounded like: a positive campaign, with deliberate choices by farmers and landowners, to let the landscape revert to its natural state.

Doing so wasn't just letting things grow where previously land had been cultivated, nor was it simply removing cattle from their pastures. To rewild properly, *all* land management had to be removed, including human intervention in things like drainage. To some people, this seemed completely *unnatural* in terms of human behaviour. Clearly, no one wanted all farmland to go wild but, Jack learned, there were real benefits in letting carefully selected areas revert to their natural state. There were even credible reports that rewilding could create jobs in the thousands – as many as twenty thousand, some people said – partly from ecotourism, but also from the careful "non-care" of large tracts of land.

First, the land would start to adapt back to the sort of plants best suited to each habitat, depending on landscape, soil type and weather. Most striking was the renewal of shrubs and trees, where previously there had been open fields. Without management, the natural plants and trees stabilising the soil in the uplands could retain more water and reduce the risk of flooding downstream; lowland fields, left to their own devices, would revert to being flood plains when necessary. Wildlife benefited too. With better ground cover, small mammals thrived and with longer grass and more trees and bushes, so did insect populations. With more trees and insects came more birds. With more birds, more seeds were spread more widely and the rewilding would snowball, sometimes surprisingly quickly. The outcome was a dramatic increase in biodiversity – along with less pollution, the key to a healthy planet.

So far as Jack could find out, the average person seemed to be in favour of rewilding, recognising that the long-term benefits to the environment outweighed any apparent loss of cultivated land. In the UK, the movement was gaining strength, with notable examples already established at the Knepp Castle Estate in Sussex, The Great Fen project in Cambridgeshire, and Carrifran Wildwood near Moffat in Dumfries and Galloway.

There were many others, Jack knew, including Coombeshead and Sharpham in Devon. In the latter, there were wild boar, beaver and water buffalo reintroduced, alongside a resurgence in many smaller mammals and amphibians. There were lots more projects across the country, some in remote areas, and some in surprisingly populated regions. The common thread with the most successful of these projects was that they were carefully planned. Rewilding wasn't just letting things go – getting it to work well meant taking many things into account. Not least, this meant thinking about the long-term consequences of radically changing the way land was used.

Getting things right, Jack thought, would get increasingly more complex as the movement gained momentum. True, there was government support, but there had to be a risk that the whole idea could become tarnished by the belief that rewilding was being *imposed* on already stressed farming communities. Many farmers denied they thought this. And it wasn't just the large landowners, but those with more modest farms also wanted it recognised that good farming and careful rewilding could go hand in hand. After all, a healthy landscape meant for greater long-term healthy and responsible farming. Getting everyone to agree on what this meant, however, might be easier said than done.

Where things became even more contentious, though, was when there was talk of reintroducing animal species that were once native but had been hunted to extinction in previous centuries. Wouldn't their return upset the current balance? Stable biodiversity requires the right plants, and smaller organisms like fungi, in the right place with the right balance of animal species too. Parachuting in apex predators could easily destroy the fragile balance as smaller mammals fought to maintain stable populations. Reintroducing animals such as lynx or wolves had to be thoughtfully done and properly prepared for.

Even then, there could always be surprises. Jack had read about the reintroduction of wolves to Yellowstone National Park in America. By 1926, wolves in the Yellowstone had been exterminated, mainly because they found domesticated cattle easy prey. Farmers sought to protect their investment and the wolves were hunted and trapped until they were no more.

What happened next took everyone by surprise, although it took years to become obvious. Without wolves to hunt them, the wild elk population kept on growing and, critically, became less mobile. In turn, this meant that they decimated new tree shoots. And with fewer trees, there were fewer birds, and with fewer trees near rivers, fewer beavers. Without beavers and their dams, streams became faster and dug their courses more quickly. Willow trees in particular struggled to grow on the banks of the now faster and more eroded streams; the bird numbers dropped still further. In a cascade of collapsing populations, the entire area lost the very biodiversity that made it special. Twenty-five years after wolves had been reintroduced, Jack read, some of the damage had been undone. Elk populations were reduced and, importantly, being ever watchful for wolves, had become much more mobile again. Willow and aspen had a better chance of growing into mature trees, songbird populations returned and with more trees to support their habitat, so did beavers. Slowly, the damage was being undone. The recovery, however, was far from complete, and it was likely that some areas would never regain the full extent of their natural diversity.

Jack wondered what this said about wolves in Scotland. If there really was a population, it would be quite small – otherwise they would have been spotted sooner. It was likely that recent rumoured sightings were the result of reduced human activity because of the Covid-19 lockdown. And if the wolves were there, and if their numbers grew, maybe the large herds of red deer would be better controlled, and in turn, the deer would do less damage to the forests, new as well as ancient. Perhaps the forests would then expand, and then *they* might support lynx and wild cats. "Perhaps" and "maybe" – there are a lot of unknowns, Jack thought. But that was why he'd set off on this adventure, to remove at least one unknown factor if he could.

***

Although Jack had come across references to rewilding as he read about wolves, his interest was further prompted by talking to the photographer, Sian Jones. Their meeting had seemed coincidental, but on reflection, perhaps not surprising.

Jack had been at the library one Saturday morning in August, returning some books. The librarian Steven was there, and they chatted about the subject. After their initial misunderstanding, they had got on quite well, and Steven had taken to dipping into some of the books that Jack borrowed – so he too was slowly building up some understanding about wolves.

This morning, he was not at the main desk, but in a side room – more of a gallery really – that was used for meetings and the occasional exhibition. Jack was at the desk handing back the books, and Steven had obviously heard his voice. He popped his head out of the gallery and gestured to Jack to come over. Finished with the returns, Jack did so.

"Come and have a look at this," said Steven. "I think you'll like it."

Jack entered the room. On the two short walls, and the long one opposite the windows, were large display boards on wheels. Another row ran down the centre of the room. On all of these were hung framed photographs of cats. The images were large, probably size A3, and there were a few even bigger ones at A2. Most were in colour, with a handful in black and white. Jack didn't know quite what he was looking at, so he said nothing.

"What do you think they are?" asked Steven.

Jack looked at the nearest image. At first glance, it could have been a normal tabby cat taking a walk in the woods, but that didn't quite fit. Yes, the cat was coloured much like a domestic tabby, but it was somewhat larger, seemed rounder, as if well-padded with flesh and fur, and its tail was much bushier, with distinct rings and a black tip. The snout looked on the short side and its ears were small. The image was crystal sharp and the colours, even though not especially bright, were rich and vibrant.

"Well, cats, obviously," smiled Jack, "but I don't quite get it. They look amazing. They're not domestic moggies, but where are they from? They're not 'big' cats, and I didn't think there were any wild cats left in the UK."

"Ah, that's because they are not. They're from Spain."

Jack wandered further in and looked at a few more pictures.

"I had no idea. Are they actual wild cats? Who took them?"

Steven explained a bit more. "It's a local photographer, Sian Jones. She's a real wildlife expert and her thing is these wild cats. She's done loads of work on them and has had a couple of big exhibitions in London and Bristol. And she's had work in *National Geographic, BBC Wildlife* and other magazines like that. These shots are all from her last trip to Spain in 2019. I'm just finishing putting things together here; captions and some explanatory texts and stuff. The exhibition opens on Thursday evening. Why don't you come along? It's free."

He dived behind one of the screens into a box on the floor. "Here's a leaflet and an invitation. Sian will be here so you can ask her all about it then." He laughed. "No more questions. I've already told you everything I know about wild cats!"

So that's what Jack did. The invitation said seven, and not wanting to miss anything, Jack timed his arrival for five to. When he got there, there were already quite a few people standing in small groups. To his surprise, this included the vet Jack knew from his previous job, and also the grey-haired woman who had brought in the fox all that time ago, and she was now accompanied by her husband. Jack said hello to the three of them and they chatted a little – he never felt "small talk" was his thing – and then Steven appeared. He was obviously enjoying his role as an unofficial master of ceremonies.

"Come and meet Sian. I've told her about your interest in wolves, and I'm sure she'd like to meet you. She can be a bit intense, you know, in a nice way, so she'll be happy to speak with someone who knows what they are talking about."

Jack doubted he could offer anything of real authority about wolves, but he did want to meet the photographer. Steven led the way to the other end of the room, right to where there were some drinks and nibbles on offer. Jack picked up a glass of orange juice. Next to the table stood a woman of about average height, probably in her mid-thirties, with dark shoulder-length hair and a pale face beneath a fringe. Jack smiled a hello and Steven introduced them.

"Jack had a sneak preview of your work the other day," he said, "and is suitably impressed."

Jack thought this was unnecessary, but he knew that what Steven said was correct. "Well, yes, they are amazing. The images are remarkable. Where did you take them?"

"Do you know Spain?" Sian replied, then continued without an answer. "I took these in northern Spain, in the Navarra region, up in the hills and mountains, but not so high as to be above the tree line. These cats like mixed and broadleaf forests, so there's good cover and also a decent amount of prey – small mammals and so on." She spoke quickly and precisely, but with unexpected pauses in her sentences, which caught Jack off guard. A couple of times he was about to speak, only to discover Sian hadn't finished.

Jack could see she knew a huge amount and was probably toning down the detail for others who, like him, knew next to nothing about wild cats.

"What do they eat?" he asked, and then felt it a silly question as she had already half answered it. Sian, however, didn't seem to mind. The explanation was quick and precise.

"Oh, small mammals mostly, like rodents, maybe squirrels… and rabbits and hares. They'll eat birds if they can catch them." Then, "Steven says you're something of an expert of wolves. That's really interesting. I don't know much about them but what interests me is the balance in ecosystems. These wild cats are a good example; they depend on the right habitat that hasn't been degraded, so they can find enough food. Plus, for wild cats, they need to be away from humans. The problem in the UK is that the few remaining wild cats have interbred with domestic cats and strays, so here the true wild cat doesn't really exist any more. They would have to be reintroduced. And finding what I've got here from Spain, just a few dozen good shots, took me a couple of months. These cats are hard to find."

She paused. "In fact, although I'm really into wild cats, it isn't so much about the cats, although of course it is that, but it's about healthy ecosystems. Without those, all these animals, wild cats, wolves, lynx, snakes, you name it, they are all in peril. And if they are, so are we."

Sian stopped. "Sorry. I tend to go on a bit. You see, I'm autistic and when I get focused on something, sometimes I have to pull myself up. When I was a child, we had cats, so I learnt everything, *everything*, there is to know about cats. Then I was given a camera for my fourteenth birthday, and I had to learn everything about cameras and photography. I'm still learning, of course, but to some people this focus looks like obsession. It's not, really. In fact, I prefer "neurodiverse" to "autistic" but people don't know what that means so I'm stuck with the word people use the most. It's a bit irritating, but I'm used to it."

Sian paused, as if to evaluate whether Jack was still listening. "But I do like to find out about things and get into the details. Mind you, I didn't realise. I didn't get a diagnosis that I was autistic until I was twenty-three. Nobody, including my schools, spotted it. I think because they don't expect girls to be autistic. Knowing has really helped. So just stop me if I'm going on." She laughed. "And tell me about wolves."

By this point Steven had moved off, and it was just Jack and Sian. Jack began to explain about how he had become interested in wolves and how he recognised and had sympathy with a passion for detail. He told her about the shepherd in Kinlochewe, and his recent trip to Torridon and Dundonnell. He began to expand on what he'd read about Yellowstone and about his idea that there might actually be wolves hiding in Scotland. Rashly perhaps, it was his turn to render himself vulnerable.

"I think I've worked out where, if they are there, they will be." He stopped, a bit embarrassed. Out in the open it sounded preposterous. But there it was, he'd said it.

Sian was quiet for a moment. "How will you *know*? How will you be *certain*? Have you tracked wild animals before? Do you think you can *prove* it one way or another?"

And there it was. The start of a plan to test Jack's idea. For them both, it was a challenge. For Jack, it would be a vindication of his reading, research and speculation. And for Sian, well, she said: "Who wouldn't want to be the first photographer in Britain to photograph secret wild wolves?"

**

Sian, Jack knew, would be on a train from Inverness that should arrive at the remote station of Garve, on the A835 to Ullapool, at 12.01 p.m. He had time to not rush, but he also had no time to waste. His own journey was about one hundred and fifty miles and might take a good three-and-a-half hours. While he didn't have to be there before her, it was obviously going to be better to arrive at about the same time. But that was assuming no hold-ups. They had booked rooms at a B & B in the village, so there was no panic about finding somewhere to camp, but the next day they would be setting out in earnest. It would be best to have plenty of time.

The morning continued fair, and the early autumn colours in the sunshine filled him with joy and optimism as he drove further into the Highlands. The sea by Fort William, and then the waters of the passing lochs, sparkled in the sun. Individual clouds cast well-defined shadows that swept across the hillsides. The light had a clarity that only comes with spring and autumn.

The roads, even at this time of year, were quite busy and it was clear that, like him, many people were taking the opportunity to snatch a few days' holiday after an arduous year and a half of Covid-19 restrictions. As he drove north, the mountains seemed to get bigger, and while Jack knew this was not uniformly the case, it all seemed quite fitting.

Jack stopped for petrol and to stretch his legs at Fort Augustus, where the Caledonian Canal enters Loch Ness. He bought a packed sandwich and a soft drink and, as a rare luxury, some crisps and a Kit-Kat. Leaving them in the car for later, he walked down to the huge lock at the end of the canal, the last of a ladder of five as the canal met the open water. Leaving the final one was a random collection of vessels: a small private yacht; a working fishing trawler just small enough to fit; and an excursions boat, full of day trippers with cameras at the ready. A nice day out, thought Jack. Perhaps on the way back, if there was time.

Jack arrived at Garve exactly four hours after leaving the campsite at Luss. He could see the station, but not reach it from the main road. He drove on, crossed the railway where it cut diagonally across the main road, drove on a bit further and then doubled back to take the road that led to the station. And there was Sian, sitting in the sun on her rucksack by the fence that marked off the local football field. The station itself was little more than two platforms, a connecting bridge and the station building – more of a house painted an optimistic Mediterranean yellow than a traditional station.

Sian was studying a map. Somehow, Jack knew that in the unlikely event of him not knowing where they were, being with Sian would mean that their chance of getting lost was negligible. She looked up as his car approached, and waved. He waved in reply and parked the car a short distance away. He walked back to where she sat.

"Hi," he said. "Good journey?"

"Not bad. Train was on time, so I've only been here twenty minutes or so. I was just about to eat some lunch."

"That sounds like a plan. If we follow this lane, it goes to the river. There might be a nice spot down there."

"OK. Let's go and see." Sian stood up and picked up her rucksack. Jack opened the car and Sian, having removed a plastic box of sandwiches and other food, placed her rucksack on the back seat, also extracting a water bottle. They got in and drove slowly towards the river. As it happened, there was no easy way to get from the road to the riverbank, but there was a wide verge on which to park nearby, so they ate standing on the long, narrow metal bridge, leaning against the girdled side and looking upstream. There was no rush, the weather was very pleasant and for Jack it was nice to stop and slow down a bit after the driving. Neither felt much need to talk, so they ate in a companionable silence.

Although very much a highland river, the Black Water was quite wide and deceptively deep. At this point it was lined on either side with mature oaks and the view of distant hills was obscured. However, they both knew that they were set for the hills and mountains north-east of this point. They looked at the map together, to go over their plan once again. An exploratory walk and a night in tents tomorrow, and then further explorations looking for clues. Next steps would be determined on a day-by-day review of what, if anything, they found.

With no need to hasten, they took their time over lunch and their discussions. Thus, it wasn't until about two that they had finished and set off to find their B & B. Given that Garve comprised about half a dozen streets only, this was not a difficult task, and the landlady had already said they could arrive any time from midday. It was relaxing to take their bags to their rooms and have nothing specific to do. Jack lay on the bed and looked again at the map and then read – he had just started Jack London's *The Call of the Wild*. Quite appropriate, he thought. Sian, he learnt later, had taken herself for a walk with her camera, capturing some striking images of the seemingly unremarkable village. Proof, he thought, if it was necessary, that this was someone with great talent and a remarkable eye for the essence of her surroundings.

***

Later, in the evening, they walked three quarters of a mile to the Garve Hotel for a bar meal. Neither drank alcohol more than occasionally, but not only was a pub meal a practical solution, it was pleasant to sit in a warm bar on a chilly evening and feel the background conversation wash over them like gentle waves at the seaside.

Sian – Jack was not surprised – was a vegetarian, so opted for a vegetable moussaka. Jack chose scampi, wondering from which ocean they had come and idly speculating on the carbon footprint of each mouthful. They chatted as they ate. Although they did not know each other well, they both realised that they would need to get on and build on the trust that they seemed to have established. So, they talked about past trips to mountains, which for Sian had been for work as well as pleasure, and about Jack's work at the animal refuge, which struck a chord with Sian.

As they ate and chatted, they became aware of a group of four men and a woman. It was difficult to tell, but they were either farmers, shepherds, foresters or a combination. One of the men seemed to be a gamekeeper. As their conversation developed, Jack and Sian talked a little less, both listening in without wishing to show that they were doing so. For their neighbours, here on a monthly get together, the conversation seemed to be about an increase in unexplained deer losses. As with the stories that Jack had heard before, some ideas were based on little more than rumour and the idea of an unexplained big cat.

"Wouldn't it be great if it was lynx?" Sian said quietly. Neither wanted to say "wolves" but it was what they were both thinking. The talk on the larger table continued, but less focused on the cause of the lost deer and more on the broader topic of predators and food chains.

"The deer really are a problem," said one of them. "Their numbers keep growing, and they have no obvious predators, especially since stalking and hunting has been off the menu during lockdown. The deer have had the best part of two seasons to multiply and the damage they're doing to what little forest we have left is serious. Even when we have deer fences, they are not foolproof, and the saplings just don't have a chance to get established."

The woman in the group spoke up. "But it's interesting. There are some areas where the deer don't go so often, and then when we find one of the carcasses, we don't see deer there again for weeks. Something strange is going on."

Her neighbour, who had been quiet so far, picked up the thread. "You know, maybe we *should* reintroduce wolves. I know you don't all like the idea, but when it's been done in Europe and the US of A, there has been an ecological benefit, long-term as well as short. You'd need a critical mass of wolves, of course, but it would definitely help manage the deer, and the risk to humans and other livestock would be very small. If the idea is sold as part of a rewilding project, or even just as a way to manage deer and rejuvenate the forests, then there could be a lot of support."

"What about the sheep?" said another.

"Well, I just don't think they are the wolf's first choice, to be honest. But probably there could be some form of compensation organised, officially. That way, any lost livestock would be part of the overall balance of costs and benefits. It would be a very small slice of the pie compared with the costs of forestry, for example. There's a lot more support for this amongst farmers and landowners than the media would have you believe. It's about a healthy balance. Wolves could easily be the best way to help that happen."

Footprints in the Mist

Jack and Sian left the B & B early the next morning and, slightly to their surprise, were weighed down with a generous packed lunch from Christine, the landlady. It didn't seem to have been in with the price, but nor had they paid extra. Perhaps, Jack thought, she had taken a liking to them, or was naturally generous – and she'd certainly seemed captivated by the few photographs Sian had shown her on one of her cameras. They'd been shots of a few of the wild cats from Spain, plus a few images from around Garve, and Christine had been taken by those too, especially as they included a couple of her own cats as well. Sian had promised to email them when she got home.

Their immediate destination was Black Bridge, a spot seven or eight miles north along the A835, where the main road crossed the Black Water River. Here, they could leave the car and follow a track further up a long valley, still heading north, before striking off on their own route. The main road followed a narrow winding valley, with wooded sides and, for the most part, was quite dark and more than a little foreboding. The day had dawned grey, but the forecast was for fair weather, so Jack hoped the clouds would break later.

The road, Jack thought, was surprisingly busy, but then he remembered it was the main route from the south to the port of Ullapool, the only substantial town for many miles.

They drove without talking, each sunk in their own thoughts. Sian had the knack of quietness, thought Jack, and she seemed content with her own company, talking when talking was useful and sometimes when she was excited by a new idea. Truth be told, this suited Jack too. He was anxious about this whole venture and was grateful that Sian seemed to take it for what it was: a walking tour to photograph wildlife, woven through with the possibility that they might, just might, find evidence of wolves still living in Britain.

The target for the day was to climb a Munro – a Scottish mountain over three thousand feet or 914.4 metres – called Am Faochagach (and pronounced, so Jack had found out, something like Am fru-hakkah) which should give them reasonable views over a large area of remote land. At 954 metres, it wasn't the highest peak in the area. That was the neighbouring Beinn Dearg, at 1,084 metres, but their chosen peak, agreed upon after quite a long discussion, should give them a better vantage point over the less precipitous land likely to be favoured by deer and, therefore, wolves.

The hills they were heading into was not the wilderness they had really hoped for, although it promised to be wild enough. On the map, there was plenty of evidence of the large estates that managed the land, with hunting lodges and cottages for foresters and gamekeepers now mostly holiday accommodation. The top of this mountain, however, should give good views for their purposes in all directions, especially to the north-east. That way, they would be looking over rough moorland and down a long valley – Gleann Beag – which itself gave access to large areas where human presence was minimal.

What did nag a little, however, was Am Faochagach's reputation as being a boggy walk. Jack had talked this through with Sian. They were planning on camping, at least for one night, so their rucksacks would be on the heavy side, and tramping uphill across wet and soggy moorland did not appeal. However, the map also showed a rough vehicle track – presumably to get hunting parties on to the hills – which should take them through the worst of it. They agreed it was worth a try. The other concern was deer stalking. The season ran until 20 October, so it was possible they might come across a shoot in action. They hoped not, and had decided to keep well clear of anything that looked like a hunting party. Perhaps, Sian had said, the pandemic would have closed down most of that sort of activity for the time being.

***

It took them half an hour or so to reach Black Bridge, find a spot to park the car and sort themselves out for the expedition. Sian seemed ready in an instant and, after many trips into the wild for her photography, had obviously fine-tuned her backpacking kit to a neat minimum, even with the extra weight of a tent and a couple of days' food. Jack's pack looked bigger and heavier but was not uncomfortable. He suspected though, that Sian would be a bit quicker and more nimble on the mountain.

They set off. Their route took them along an estate track, graded, but in good condition. About three kilometres up the valley, there would be a bridge by a weir. From there, they could cut almost due west up the hillside. It would be steep to start with, but then they would gain a broad ridge. By walking more or less due north, they would skirt round a wood and join the deer stalkers track – that at least was the plan.

As promised, the sky did look as if the cloud would break, and by the time they were committed to the ascent, the grey had turned to white, and patches of blue could be seen in growing gaps. There was little wind, just a gentle breeze, and late September or not, it was turning into a warm day. Jack, who had kept pace with Sian quite easily in the valley, began to drop behind.

This didn't bother either of them. They each had a map and compass, plus GPS devices, and they had agreed several points before the summit where they could wait if they became separated. Each in their own company, they made steady progress up the hillside. An hour after leaving the car, they had reached the ridge. Sian seemed in her element and Jack, who was also reasonably fit, was enjoying the steady pace, a sense of good progress and the wide-open spaces.

They had already come a good distance and gained some height, but Jack was reminded again just how big the Scottish hills could be. The mountains spread in all directions, interspersed with the glens, lochs and forest. The hills themselves had taken on the tinges of autumn. Patches of heather clung on to some bloom and the grass had begun to yellow. The clouds were now broken and patchy. Sun streamed through the gaps, and another, lower, layer of clouds was developing – also broken and wispy, but now touching the nearby peaks, which danced in and out of the slowly moving mist.

Sian was waiting for him ahead and Jack took the chance to look around and orient himself. After a short break, they moved on. It was warm in the sun and Jack had already taken several large mouthfuls of water from his bottle. Unwilling to add too much weight to his pack, he had limited himself to just two separate litre bottles and now the first was nearly empty. They would be far from clean-running streams for most of the day, so he resolved to be more disciplined and ration his water.

On they walked, at a steady pace. Once again, Sian crept ahead. And again, neither worried. They would meet at the summit in no more than a couple of hours, and at that point, they could take stock and decide where they might be best off looking for signs of deer and then of wolves.

Jack stopped to take a photograph and noted that Sian was now a good five hundred metres ahead, moving deceptively quick along the track. It wasn't much of a track really – not as neatly defined as the map had suggested – but it served them well. It steered them neatly though the worst of the boggy ground that sat on the ridge. Re-shouldering his pack, Jack could see wisps of cloud rolling towards where he stood. Looking ahead, a finger of cloud had already slipped between himself and Sian. Jack double-checked his position and did his best to ignore his thirst. He walked on, following the track and taking note of what he could see, as a point of reference if visibility disappeared completely.

As he tramped, the cloud closed in. It wasn't the dark and heavy cloud of rain and storm, and it hardly even felt damp. Looking straight up he could see blue sky, but ahead the mist was bright, almost dazzling, and increasingly opaque. Sian had disappeared completely.

***

Jack continued, conscious of his thirst and aware that he was still several hours away from finding a stream. As the ridge gained height, the ground underfoot began to change. Yes, it was still damp in places, but there were now outcrops of rock and areas too of bare earth, which seemed to have dried a bit. Sometimes, it was difficult to tell the difference, and more than once he wobbled, stepping on to a rock, only to discover it gave way beneath him as the soil crumbled under his boot.

By now, the track had crested a false summit and had petered out. The ridge was flatter for a while and Jack realised he should now be about a kilometre from the real summit. In front of him, the ground rose gently to a point marked on the map as 844 metres. Just another hundred metres or so of vertical distance to go. He took his rucksack off, placing it carefully next to a tussock of grass and relishing the lightness of his step without the extra weight. He was so thirsty!

A little way off was a patch of rock, shining slightly in the diffuse light. As he moved, the shine became a dazzle. Water! He walked over and had a look. What he thought was rock was hard, compressed earth. Quite recently, it had probably been muddy and glutinous. Now it was firm and springy, and into it were pressed a series of puddles filled with crystal clear water – puddled dew or the remnants of a shower.

The water was irresistible. Jack got down on his knees and had a closer look. Then he stood up, as if stunned. He looked again. The puddles weren't just depressions in the soil. They were footprints. No, not footprints. They were paw prints. The paw prints of a wolf! Of this Jack was certain. He had looked at so many illustrations, and it was one of the things he had hoped to find on his trip to Torridon. Speechless – even without an audience – he took the few paces back for his camera and returned to take several photographs. Had Sian seen these? He guessed not, or she would have waited.

This was amazing. He tried not to get too excited. What else could it be? Surely there was nothing else that could have made these marks. Even the biggest hunting dog would not have left such a clear record. Anyway, did people hunt with dogs these days? And would they have brought them up here? He stopped taking pictures and just stared at the prints. Then he got out the map and his GPS. He made several checks to get as accurate a fix as possible on his location, and then marked it on the map and as a waypoint in the GPS mapping app.

Slowly, he got up and forced himself to be calm. He sorted out his pack and looked at the empty water bottle. He knew he should wait to find a running stream, but he really was parched! He stepped over to the wolf prints again, knelt down and sipped the water from them. It was clear. It tasted fine. More than that, it was cool and refreshing. Mentally, he crossed his fingers, hoping there would be no ill effects.

***

As agreed, Sian was waiting for Jack at the summit. Mist and cloud blew gently across the mountain, so as he approached the cairn, Sian came in and out of view. Finally, he got there. He didn't know what to say.

"There's… prints. There are paw prints. I'm certain they're wolf prints. I really think they are. You've got to come and look!"

Sian stared at him. "You're joking! Are you sure? Could it be anything else?"

Jack shook his head. He was hot, still thirsty and was struggling to get his thoughts in order. "You've got to look. They're not far."

He shook off his pack and took out the map. "I've marked the spot. It's about ten minutes' walk going down; about twenty on the way back up to here, less without our rucksacks. They're a bit off the obvious line to walk. I thought they were puddles at first and I was really thirsty, and I know you're not supposed to, but I was going to sip the water." He pointed to his empty bottle. "Then I saw what they were. I took some photographs."

"Oh, why didn't you say? Show me!"

Jack took out the camera and handed it over. He sat down and waited for her comment.

"I think you're right! Come on. We can leave the packs here. Bring the map!"

She jumped up, her own camera in hand and thrust Jack's back at him. "Let's go!" And off she shot, bounding down the slope. Jack launched himself to his feet and followed, laughing as he ran.

"Slow down," he called. "We don't want to twist an ankle or anything daft."

And Sian stopped and turned round. She was laughing too. "OK. Show me the way." And then she asked, "Did you drink from the footprints?"

Jack was embarrassed. "Well, I was *really* thirsty!"

"Forget *thirst*," laughed Sian. "You do know what happens when you drink from a wolf's paw print?"

She looked at Jack's blank face and laughed again. He shrugged.

"So…" she looked at him as if to check whether he was listening. "Just watch out for a full moon!" She laughed again. "It's supposed to turn you into a werewolf!" And with that, she took the map from his hand, turned and strode off downhill.

***

By the time they were back at the summit, it was early afternoon. To Jack's relief, they were both satisfied that the prints had been wolf-made. They sat at the summit cairn and ate lunch, discussing their plan of action. The weather seemed to be holding and the clouds seemed to be higher, so visibility was not a concern.

They decided to keep watch and invest time in waiting. So, fed and watered – Jack had allowed himself a couple of mouthfuls from his second water bottle – they made their way down the gentle northern upper slopes of the mountain. About halfway down was a short spur. From this point, it looked as if they would get a clear view both up and down large sections of Gleann Beag. And Sian said she thought she had seen a herd of deer in the upper reaches of the glen earlier. If they could follow its movements, perhaps they could pick up evidence of predators.

Sure enough, Sian had been right. For a couple of hours, using their binoculars and Sian sometimes with her camera, they scanned the landscape – hills, valleys, lochans, corries. Then Sian saw the deer again.

A herd of about forty were grazing on the shoulder this side of the U-shaped valley that made up the head of the glen. They must have been moving gradually along the valley side and had only just come back into view as they rounded a corner. A large stag seemed pre-eminent and he, with other larger animals, was not only choosing the path, but also keeping his head up, eyes and ears alert. Natural behaviour, Jack presumed, and everything seemed quite relaxed.

He swung his binoculars to the east and got another surprise. Across the valley was an animal carcass. It was further away than the one he'd seen in Torridon, but it was strikingly similar, even down to the location on an outcrop of rock. Another kill? He pointed it out to Sian. She looked at it for several minutes, saying nothing.

At last, she spoke. "It really could be, couldn't it?"

Half an hour later, the herd of deer was still there, making its way south-east in parallel to the valley floor. Then, panic!

Without warning, the whole herd was on the move. This was not just a false alarm, the sort when a large animal is panicked by the flapping of a bird breaking cover. This was real, purposeful and urgent. In front of the herd was a ravine and a series of waterfalls. Below them, the slope was steep but of consistent gradient and running to open grass, so, very manageable for the deer, but that seemed to be where the trouble was coming from. Above them, the slope lessened, and if they doubled back on themselves, they would reach a gently inclined plateau, with cliffs on two sides but a wide open space which would eventually get them back down to the upper glen.

Up they charged, seemingly in silence and as one. They ran as only hunted animals can run. Single-minded and desperate, but sure-footed and determined.

For Sian and Jack, it was like watching a movie. Neither said a word. They were spellbound. And then, after what seemed like hours but was less than ten minutes, the deer stopped running. The stag and a couple of others turned, panting, and surveyed the broad corrie up which they had come. Were they satisfied of safety? It was impossible to tell. But for the moment, they seemed to think so. The two humans scanned their fields of vision, with and without binoculars, but could see nothing out of the ordinary.

Sian broke the silence. "Amazing. What was that?"

Jack knew what he wanted it to be, but even now he hardly dared say it. Instead, he came down to earth. "It's getting late. We've an hour or so of light left. We should camp. Down there." He pointed left, to the west. "Down there by the loch – Loch Prille it says on the map – and we can explore a bit more tomorrow."

Sian looked at him, as if surprised by Jack's decisiveness, then nodded. "You're right, and that looks like a good spot. And it will be good to move a bit again."

So off they went, stiff from sitting, walking for just a relatively short descent of a kilometre or so. In fading light, they pitched tents near the loch. In front of them, on the other side of the water, was a great pyramid of rock, the peak of Cona' Mheall. To their right were the precipitous cliffs of Cnap Coire Loch Tuath, now a deep and sombre grey in the dusk.

"Tomorrow," Jack suggested, "perhaps we should explore the other side of the glen. We could leave the tents here and just go with a bit of food and waterproofs – and cameras of course!"

Sian nodded. "Yes, that makes sense. Whatever spooked the deer today didn't come from this side."

***

The next morning, the weather seemed like the day before. A grey covering of high cloud, which, in time with their early morning cooking, seemed to be slowly waking to the new day. After breakfast, and after checking they had put everything securely in the tents ("Who knows who or what will pass by," said Sian), they set off.

It turned out to be a long day. It took them sustained walking to descend into Gleann Beag, following it east and downstream. They crossed the river by a recently rebuilt girder bridge by a weir and then backtracked to the spot where they had seen the carcass.

It looked as if it had been dead for several weeks. Largely stripped of flesh, the shape and the remains of the telltale reddish-brown colouring confirmed it was a deer – although the antlers made the question academic. It was difficult to tell how old the animal had been, but the antlers had six points. "Number and size are not a guarantee of age, especially in the wild," Sian said. On two of them were small clumps of animal hair. Instead of the deer's own colours, the hair was a mixture of a rich greyish-brown with hints of amber. The individual hairs were long, and the fairer ones were surprisingly soft.

Jack rummaged in his pack for a tissue and a spare plastic bag. "I'm going to take this back and find someone who can tell us what it's from." He picked it from the antler and held it to his nose. "Mmm… smells of wet dog!"

A little later, they returned to the bridge and picked up a path which climbed steeply to a hidden patch of water – Loch Sruban Mora. There, they rested. Either side of them were rough, rocky hillsides. Ahead, a gap enticed them northwards and gradually downhill, which took them to a wasteland of broken rock, rough grass and heather, and many lochans interspersed with bog. Beyond that was an impenetrable barrier of steep cliffs which plunged down to a glen below. They turned and retreated uphill and south, to a top above the hidden loch. It was good to sit down and look at the map.

There they stayed for an hour or so. Sian scanned the horizon with her binoculars and took photographs; Jack did the same, but without the passion of the previous day. He switched to studying the map. Sian looked over his shoulder.

"What are you thinking?" he asked.

"I'm thinking that if there are wolves near here, they need a lair. And if you ask me, they'll want trees. There's no real forest for a long way, but there is this." She pointed at the map, to a spot a couple of kilometres from where they sat. "It's a sheltered patch of woodland on the crag side.

Plenty of protection, and maybe even a cave or two. But it's impossible to get to from here. It's surrounded by near vertical rock on three sides, but we could get at it from the north if we drove round and then walked in. What do you think?"

Jack had been looking at the same area, but Sian had summarised it perfectly.

"Yes, that's good. And here." He pointed at a single building by a loch to the north-west. "Here is a bothy. It's supposed to be in good condition, so we wouldn't have to take tents."

Sian nodded. "OK. That's a plan. Let's move. We'll get back to the tents today and walk out in the morning. We can probably be there, at the bothy, by this time tomorrow."

A New Era

The next morning, their descent back to the car took longer than expected. From the wild campsite, the first section was precipitous, time consuming, and, for Jack at least, quite scary. At the southern end of Loch Prille, by which they had camped, was a waterfall where the loch emptied over the corrie wall into a precipitous glaciated valley. The waterfall itself wasn't a single huge drop; rather, it was an initial vertical fall, followed by a series of cascades down a steep and rocky hillside. In places, the water streamed over long sloping slabs. Elsewhere, it plunged into pools and through boulders and over a myriad of shorter drops. Overall, it was too dangerous to cross, even on the fine day it was turning out to be.

Thus, Sian and Jack were committed to the steep eastern bank. It wasn't clear where they would be able to cross, and their progress downhill was slow and uncomfortable. Jack regretted not having thought about this the day before, when they could have pitched camp on the other side of the loch. A slip here and a broken ankle or a cracked skull would be a worrying probability.

It took a long time to travel the near full kilometre of unpleasant downhill scrambling before finding a good place to cross. Once over, the ground was less hostile and they were able to make steady progress down Coire Làir. But here though, even Sian wasn't fast. The narrow valley was pathless and the ground underfoot was rough and uneven. With heavy rucksacks, it paid to take care. As they walked, Jack contemplated the next stage in the search for wolves. Unsettled by the earlier steep descent and overtaken by pessimism, he felt that yesterday's footprints may not have been *Canis lupus* after all.

Gradually, they continued along the shore of another long loch and below that, across rough heathland which, bisected by two rivers, threatened to be wet as well. Indeed, there was no choice but to cross one of the rivers. Despite the lack of recent heavy rain, it was still fast enough to take seriously, so they headed for a spot where it was split by several small islands. They made it across with dry feet. After that, they picked up a path which took them at long last to the main road by the bridge at Torran Dubh. They were not far from the head of Loch Glascarnoch, which dominated the valley.

Jack stopped a few metres from the roadside and was glad to drop his rucksack. He rummaged for a snack and drank some water. Sian did the same.

"That's about nine kilometres we've walked. It's another ten to the car – with our packs, that's at least two hours, probably more. It's a good six miles. We'll not make it to the bothy any time today."

Sian nodded. "Let's look at the map."

Together, they considered their options. There were two obvious routes to Coiremore Bothy. The shorter looked about fifteen kilometres; the longer possibly half that again, if not more. On both routes, much of the journey would be on substantial tracks and well-used paths. Jack pointed at the only town visible on the map. Ullapool.

"This isn't big but there's quite a lot there. A proper town. And there's a campsite on the point, and look – it looks like we could hire mountain bikes. Chances are we could cycle all the way to the bothy."

Sian was thinking. "OK. Not sure about bikes though. If we get a flat or something breaks, we'll be worse off. Let's get to Ullapool and the campsite and think about the weather."

She looked at her watch. Eleven thirty.

"And we'd best get walking. If there's a bus going in our direction, it's bound to have passed here already. And we'll be lucky to get a lift."

So, they shouldered their rucksacks. In a gesture towards the Highway Code, they crossed the road to face the traffic, and set off. The walking was easy, but a bit of a trudge along the tarmac. If they got into a rhythm, Jack assumed, it wouldn't be too bad.

And so they walked on. A few cars passed in the opposite direction and they resigned themselves to the full ten kilometre walk.

After half an hour, Sian stopped. "Listen." It was a vehicle behind them. From the sound of it, a van or truck. They waited. Around a gentle bend in the road, where trees touched the loch side, sure enough, there it was, a Land Rover making steady progress towards them. "You never know your luck." She smiled and held up her arm in a wave.

The vehicle pulled up. It wasn't new but it was clean and well maintained. It was a typical Land Rover, green, and generally unexceptional, except for yellow lettering on the side: Creag Ruadh Estate. The driver lowered the window and half laughed.

"You'll not be tramping along here for fun. Jump in and I'll take you down the road. Where are you heading?"

Sian beamed. "The end of the loch. Black Bridge. That would be great."

Jack agreed. "Thanks," he said. "That would be perfect."

So in they got, rather clumsily with packs, and smiled their appreciation. They set off. The driver didn't introduce himself but congratulated them on choosing fine weather. He didn't otherwise enquire about their adventures. It was obvious, after all, that they had been in the hills, and no doubt he was pre-occupied with his own business. And the journey, now they were no longer walking, was quickly over. Soon, they passed the winter snow gates by the inn and a few minutes later, pulled up by Jack's car.

They clambered out with their rucksacks. "Thank you, again," Jack said. "We really appreciate the lift."

"No problem," was the reply. "Take care, wherever you're off to next. It's been a funny year."

Jack seized the sudden opportunity. "It has. But is there anything we should look out for?"

The driver gave him a strange look. "Well, you look like you know these are hills to respect. Obviously, don't do anything daft that puts other people at risk coming out to find you. But other than that, something's attacking the deer in the remoter glens, so keep your eyes open and give them a wide berth or you might get caught up in that too."

Sian interrupted. "We're heading to Coiremore Bothy. Are things all right up there?"

"Oh yes – you'll be fine. Just keep your eyes open. My new laird…" – he spoke as if he couldn't quite bring himself to mean the title – "he owns the land up there. The real threat is his big dog." He smiled. "So long."

They waved him goodbye and the Land Rover pulled off on to the road and was soon gone.

"Come on," said Jack. "Let's have something to eat."

***

While they ate, they spread the map on the bonnet of the car and looked again at the two routes into the bothy.

"Bikes are tempting," said Sian, "but I'd rather walk."

Jack was about to remonstrate – he was quite keen on the relative speed of cycling – but Sian explained. "Like I said, if something goes wrong, it'll be a pain, and we'll have rucksacks, not pannier bags, so we'll be top heavy on bumpy tracks. I don't want to risk coming off and damaging the cameras." And that, Jack realised, was that.

"OK," he said. "We can walk. And anyway, we won't have tents. We can take food for three days and still not be overloaded. Let's get to Ullapool and sort ourselves out."

***

It was a relaxed afternoon exploring the town and stocking up on food. They had found the campsite easily enough and sorted out their gear for an early start. It was handy not to be carrying tents, and although they automatically packed waterproofs, the good weather forecast gave them confidence. By eight the next morning, they had left the campsite and by eight thirty, had parked in a lay-by on the shores of Loch Broom. The map showed the nearby gathering of cottages marked as Campbelltown.

From here, a forestry track climbed the mountainside through a wooded valley. The main stream, out of sight but not out of hearing, ran close to the track to begin with, but soon took its own route, an invisible constant roar at the bottom of a ravine. The track was steep too, and they walked in silence, each with their own thoughts, attempting to establish a rhythm as they made snail-like progress up the incline.

After about a kilometre, and having climbed a good two hundred metres, the track emerged from the woods on the shoulder of a hill. The gradient began to ease, and after another hundred metres of ascent, the track was more or less level. Ahead, it went uphill again, but the worst of the climb was behind them.

From this point, the route should be straightforward, albeit not quite a walk in the park. The track followed a narrow valley, Srath Nimhe, which ran beneath broken crags on both sides. At the other end, it popped out into the Achall valley, their main access route to the bothy. Even in the bright morning, however, it seemed a foreboding place. Eventually, the track would become a footpath and descend across open moorland before dropping down to work its way round the grounds of a country house. This, they had realised, was the old Victorian shooting lodge now known as Creag Ruadh Lodge – it was the epicentre of the Creag Ruadh Estate and no doubt the home of yesterday's friendly Land Rover.

Behind the lodge was a footbridge which would carry them across the Achall River. Once over, they could follow a succession of tracks and paths all the way to the bothy, a walk of another six kilometres or so with plenty of steady uphill across moor and mountainside. Not a difficult walk, but not one to rush. With good fortune, and a couple of stops included, they should reach their destination in the early afternoon.

***

The tramp along Srath Nimhe passed without incident, but both Jack and Sian were glad as the landscape opened out and they were free of the oppressive slopes that had hemmed them in along the valley. As they made their way north-east, the path wound its way through waist-high heather, broad sweeps of now browning grass, and eventually through stands of trees. Jack had to admit to himself that he could name very few. There were certainly some oaks, and some mountain ash, plus the occasional Scots pine, resplendent with their pink-tinged bark, but other varieties he could not name. He smiled to himself. Sian would almost certainly know.

Further ahead, the views opened up completely. On the other side of the glen were the cliffs of Creag Ruadh, from which the estate took its name. Some distance behind stood the conical peak of Cnoc Damh. At six hundred metres high, it was not an enormous mountain, but it was still very distinct. Further to the right were the dark crags above their destination, Coire Mòr, and the big mountains behind. If their thinking was right, that would be a good spot for the wolves if they were there. While quite close to humans, it was not a busy spot, and wolves living on this side would have access to several glens and the intervening mountains – and in particular to the several herd of deer that roamed these open spaces. Still apprehensive about the whole project, Jack couldn't decide whether he wanted to find the wolves or not.

The last part of the descent behind them, Jack and Sian followed the path as it skirted round the lodge. Built in the Victorian mock gothic style, it was constructed of gloomy grey stone and boasted a selection of towers and turrets. In the sunshine and surrounded by lawns, it looked impressive, and Jack could imagine it would be decorated to match inside, no doubt with a number of stag heads on the walls and huge open fireplaces to keep the damp and cold away in the dark months of winter.

The path kept the house to the left and negotiated a stand of half a dozen Scots pine to the right, before leading straight on to the footbridge, suspended as it was between two stone piers. Steps led up to the one on their side. The bridge itself hung on cables some twenty feet above the river and it was swaying a little in the breeze. It was narrow and only really wide enough to go in single file in comfort. They hadn't stopped walking since leaving the car, and it was time for a break. Sian spoke first, putting into words exactly what Jack was thinking.

"Let's get over the river and carry on for half a mile. Once we're away from the house, we can stop and have a rest. We should double check the route."

Jack nodded. They arrived at the bridge. Again, Sian spoke – this time with a flash of humour. "You go first. You know, in case it breaks."

Jack laughed. "If you say so!" He grabbed the cables, which acted as handrails, and started to climb. Five steps up and he was on the platform at the top of the pier. Ahead, the bridge hung in a long shallow curve, with wooden planks forming the floor. Two steel hawsers continued as handrails; from them, more cables came down vertically to support the planking underfoot. Jack took a hesitant step. He took another and then his whole weight was on the bridge and he was moving – not quickly, but steadily, and he decided the most comfortable thing was to keep going. The bridge, of course, was fine. It wobbled a bit, but it had been designed to do so, and soon, Jack was in the middle of the span, then making his way up and to the pier on the other side. A change in the movement of the bridge told him Sian had started to cross, but he didn't look back.

As Jack came to the end, he could see there was someone there, waiting. They were off to one side, and Jack didn't take a close look until he climbed down, backwards, because of the bulk of his pack. At the bottom, he turned. In front of him was a strange concoction. From the feet up, an expensive pair of green wellies, jeans (probably expensive), a waxed cotton jacket, open to show a red woollen jumper (that looked expensive too, like the twill shirt), and a flat cap that somehow said "country sports" rather than "life at t'mill". Under the cap, an expressionless, fashionably unshaven face. To the man's left was a dog. A very big dog indeed, standing alert and on a very tight leash. Its black and tan colouring, upright pointed ears, inscrutable eyes and enormous jaws screamed one thing: Dobermann.

Jack looked back at the face. He had recognised him in an instant. And it wasn't just that this laird was on TV three times a week; Jack would have known him anywhere. It was Martin Grough. The school bully and Jack's tormentor of his youth, the last person he ever wanted to see again, and absolutely the last person he wanted to see here. Jack hoped, desperately, that Martin wouldn't recognise him.

No such luck. Martin laughed. "Why, it's Jack. It is, isn't it? Yes, Jack Green. Jack Green the—"

Martin stopped mid-sentence. Sian had appeared at the top of the pier. She said nothing but turned and started the descent. Martin looked up at her and watched her closely as she climbed down the steps, "and Jack's friend... Hello, and welcome. Jack, you must introduce me." Martin's smile was quite neutral, but somehow managed to seem menacing.

Jack was lost for words, but before Martin could speak again, Sian got in before him.

"Hello. Do you two know each other?"

"This is Martin Grough," said Jack, by way of pointless explanation.

"Yes, I know," replied Sian. "He's on TV." Then to Martin she said: "Do you own this land?"

Jack was encouraged to see that Martin was temporarily thrown – but not for long. Presumably, he had plenty of practice at awkward conversations. Martin turned and directed a creepy smile at Sian.

"Oh, yes. We're old friends, aren't we, Jack? Old friends from school. We go back a long way... but who are you? Jack, you must introduce us!"

"I'm Sian. So, you really own this estate. It's a fantastic part of the country."

Knowing how hard Sian found forced social encounters, Jack was impressed. She had obviously decided to counter Martin's false pleasantries with her own.

"Well, yes," replied the laird. "I bought it last year and now I'm loving it. And it's nice to have some visitors. And it's nice to meet you, Sian. Any friend of Jack's is a friend of mine. Where are you two off to, if I may be so impertinent on my own land?"

Now it was Jack's turn. "Oh, just up to the bothy. A bit of walking. Fresh air."

Martin smirked, as if somehow, he'd caught Jack out. "Ah, Magoo's Bothy. That will be lovely. Weather's changing tomorrow, but that won't matter." He laughed again. "You'll be nice and cosy up there out of the rain. It's very romantic, up there all alone."

Neither Jack nor Sian said a word. It just didn't seem worth it. Jack for one, wanted to get away.

"Anyway, mustn't keep you. Got to be going. But take care. You'll be a long way from civilisation up there. And something's getting the deer, so watch out." He grinned, enjoying himself. "And if you're coming back this way, be careful here too. Young Frodo…" – Martin yanked on the dog's lead – "young Frodo gets out occasionally, and he knows it's his land too, and he's very possessive."

And with that, Martin walked between them straight to the steps, let out some of the lead, saw that it was enough for the dog to bound up and then quickly followed the animal up himself. Halfway across the bridge, he turned and shouted back, in a voice that could hardly have been more patronising, "So long. Do take care!"

***

Sian turned to Jack. "What…?"

Jack could hardly speak. "I'll tell you later. Come on. Let's go."

Forty-five minutes later, they were still walking. The track, running east at this point, had gained height again and they could now see a long stretch of water ahead – Loch an Daimh. They'd have to turn south at the foot of the loch and start another long uphill section. After a long morning, they needed a rest and at the brow of a short rise, they saw a large flat boulder by the side of the track. They made for it without speaking, unslung their rucksacks and sat down.

It seemed to Jack as if all his strength had left him. Sian said nothing and busied herself with finding food and her water bottle. She ate, sipped water and looked at the view. For about five minutes, Jack just sat there, also looking at the view but not really seeing it.

Eventually, he too took up his water bottle and had a sip. He got out some food – a cheese sandwich made that morning – and took a bite.

After a couple of minutes, he spoke.

"That was Martin Grough. I'd sort of forgotten how much I don't like him. And I thought he might have changed, but he's still the same vicious bully but now he's older and cleverer at it! And everyone likes him. It's just so wrong!"

Sian nodded. "Did you really go to school with him?"

Jack nodded. "He made it a misery. Not just for me, of course, for others too."

Sian looked at him sideways. "But mainly for you?"

"Well, that's what it felt like." Jack looked at Sian, then back at the distant mountains. For about ten minutes he spoke, trying to summarise for Sian the history of his childhood and, in particular, the huge sense of relief he felt when he and Martin had gone their different ways.

For several long moments, Sian said nothing. Then she nodded. "I went to several schools. Some were brilliant. They'd really notice what was going on and do something about it. And some were a bit rubbish and didn't care. And even the good ones didn't understand everything. Life would have been a lot easier if my teachers had worked out, I was autistic. I don't think I blame them as such. My parents didn't see it either. But someone should have asked the right questions and they didn't. But the thing is, they never expected girls to be autistic. Not sure why, really. There are loads of neurodiverse people and lots are women, including some who are really successful. Maybe they just don't let it define them, so people don't notice. But at some schools, well, they should be more aware.

"Anyway, so me and another girl, who wasn't even my friend but was like me, just had to work out how to do things to fit in. It was really, really tiring trying to understand how things worked, how other *people* worked. I read and read, and watched loads and loads of wildlife documentaries. I thought if I understood animals, I might understand people more easily too. Not sure if that worked, of course. And in the end, a lot of it was hit-and-miss." She looked at her water bottle. "But then I also learned to look, *really look*, probably better than most people. And now I can sell pictures to *National Geographic*, so it wasn't all bad." She laughed. "Come on. We've still got to get to the bothy."

***

As they knew it was going to be, it was quite a long walk, with several river crossings. They made a note to take care of rising waters if it rained. Although their route followed a track all the way, they made several stops to take sightings with their maps and compasses and compared their calculated locations with the position given by their GPS units. They were pleased that the results matched. Despite Martin's comment, they did not expect terrible weather, but it was clear it would be easy to get lost if they had poor visibility on the return journey.

The peaks, cliffs and corries above their destination they had seen for a long while, and for ages it seemed as if they were not getting any closer at all. They were glad, therefore, finally, to come within sight of Loch a' Choire Mhòir. The bothy was about halfway along its length and the final half mile was on more or less level ground. Jack felt in definite need of rest, and even Sian had lost some of the spring in her step.

As they approached, details started to appear. First, an upturned boat at the near end of the grey stone building. It was a long, low structure, in good order and overlooking the loch to the west. There were two chimney stacks – one at an angle – with a modern corrugated roof. The windows were shuttered but, as they got closer, they could see smaller windows set into the end of the building and skylight windows in the roof. By the time they reached it properly, it was obvious that this was a substantial and sturdy building. As they were to discover, it was three separate accommodations, really very simple bunkhouses, all in the same building but not connected. Above the first door was the legend, MAGOO'S BOTHY, carved into a polished granite slab.

"I read about this place," said Jack. "It's named after a soldier who was killed in Kosovo in 2001, I think. He was with the peacekeeping force. He loved the hills and staying in these remote huts. His family and friends rebuilt this place to commemorate him."

He pulled the bolt back and pushed the door open. "Let's drop our rucksacks here and have a look around."

So, that's what they did. The next section was smaller, a single room, with a table, stove and sleeping platform. The third part was the official Coiremor Bothy, one of the many in the Mountain Bothies Association network. It was two rooms, one for cooking and sitting – the presence of a couple of sofas was proof you could get here in a 4x4 – and a second for sleeping, again with raised wooden platforms. They went back to Magoo's and explored inside. Here, there were two rooms: one just for sleeping; and the larger with a fireplace, a sofa, work surfaces for cooking and, along one wall, another sleeping platform. A framed notice told the story of Mark "Magoo" Maguire and another notice, the Bothy Code, set out the guidelines for using the property.

Sian spoke. "This is pretty good. Looks like it's quite well used. Hope the people don't put off the wolves."

This had been Jack's thought too. "Well, we can but see. Let's sort ourselves out and think about the best places to look."

So, they unpacked their rucksacks and settled in. Jack tidied the work surfaces to make room for their own stoves, while Sian took her rucksack into the second room. Jack put his own sleeping bag out on the platform near the fireplace. He looked at his watch. Four. He called through: "I might just walk up the loch and take a look."

"OK," came the reply. "I'll see you in a bit."

Outside, he stood and surveyed his surroundings. Opposite the bothy was a sharp peak, Creag an Duine, which, from this angle, looked as if it had a razor-sharp ridge leading to the summit. But it was not isolated. Rather, it was the summit promontory from the great sweep of cliffs and corries that formed a larger mountain. From the map, this is what Jack hoped held promise for their search. The valley in which he now stood was remote enough, but once on the tops, any sure-footed animal would have the range of rounded hills which sat above the glens. Wolves here could travel for miles in many directions, not always away from humans, but certainly out of sight most of the time.

He walked towards the head of the loch, where he could see a narrow sandy beach. Beyond, the flat valley floor continued rising gently for another half mile before the slopes steepened sharply and quickly, and became crags and cliffs. What they needed was a good lookout point from where they could see below, but also have an idea of what was going on, on the tops. If the weather held, he thought, they could get to the top of the ridge behind the bothy. From there, they could look along this whole valley and also across to the rolling tops beyond. Fingers crossed for the weather, then.

***

That evening, they cooked on their stoves and by the light of head torches, scrutinised the maps for the umpteenth time. When all the permutations were exhausted, they sat and talked through what they might do if they did see wolves. Jack had assumed that Sian's priority would be to photograph them. He wasn't wrong, she explained, but what really got her excited was the prospect of seeing them for real, and the closer the better.

"Just to see them here would be amazing. After all these years, after all the stories of how terrible wolves are, it would just be fantastic to see them and show people that is not the case."

Jack agreed. "They've got such a bad reputation. It would be good to show they could really make a contribution to biodiversity. Given enough space, they could really enrich the land and the landscape. They've usually been the bad guys. Just think of all the fairy tales. *Little Red Riding Hood, The Three Little Pigs, Peter and the Wolf,* the *Legend of Gelert…* there must be loads more. And the wolf is mostly bad – although, interestingly, that is not always the case in Irish myth and legend. It's complex stuff, trying to unpick the way in which people have been fascinated by wolves, almost as if their dog/non-dog nature is full of contradictions."

There was wood and kindling by the fire but they hadn't lit it. It wasn't cold yet, plus they'd seen that they were supposed to replace what they used. The only patch of trees nearby clung to cliffs at the head of the valley, and they doubted it would produce enough fallen branches to be of use. They had found a plentiful supply of candles though, so had lit a couple.

In the flickering light, Sian nodded. "It's not surprising. For thousands of years, humans and wolves have been in competition. And when your competition is as fierce and strong as a wolf, and when they might eat your animals, they're just going to get a bad reputation, but it's going to be more subtle than black and white, good and evil.

"And they've always been clever, too. I mean, in *Little Red Riding Hood*, the wolf is pretty cunning – and nearly gets away with it. Even the ancient Greeks and Romans regarded them as vicious and bloodthirsty, but they couldn't quite get rid of the idea that wolves may be part of balance in the world. After all, Romulus and Remus, who founded Rome, were abandoned; then they were saved by a she-wolf who suckled them like her own cubs."

Jack remembered what Sian had said about drinking from a wolf's paw print. "Not to mention werewolves," he said. "They get a really bad press! I mean, always killing and causing chaos. Real Jekyll and Hyde characters who can't control their worst urges. And they've been part of folklore for centuries. There are lots of medieval tales. In one of them, a hunter fights off a wolf and, in the process, cuts off one of the wolf's paws. On his way home, he goes a little out of his way to visit a wealthy friend to show him his trophy. But, when he unwraps it, it isn't a paw. It's a woman's hand, and on one of the fingers is a ring. They are both shocked, but his friend is frantic with worry. He's recognised the ring. Immediately, he goes to find his wife and discovers her bandaging the stump of an arm with no hand. It was her who was the wolf and, of course, she has no choice but to admit being a werewolf, even though she knows she'll get burnt at the stake as a result."

Sian picked up on the idea. "Well, as you say, wolves go right back to the classics, and re-emerge in European folklore in Norse legend. But you're right. Werewolves get a bad press, and, of course, now they're wrapped up in horror stories and are all the more frightening because they *are* part human. In some ways, the old stories were simpler and less like horror movies. I remember a tale from a childhood storybook. It's almost the opposite of yours, because a mysterious wolf saves the human. Once upon a time – they all started like this – an abbot was travelling home, but he wasn't a very pious man and he was drunk after a good lunch with the local squire. He fell off his pony and hit his head. He lay there unconscious, and the blood attracted some ferocious wild cats. They were about to attack him when a wolf came to the man's rescue and drove off the cats. Somehow, the wolf woke the abbot and then escorted him back to the monastery, so no harm would come to him. But the next day, the priest had a surprise visitor, another priest who worked for the most important bishop in the country. Well, *he* had been the werewolf. The abbot got a huge telling off for being such a bad example. He was demoted and another, holier, man was made abbot in his place."

Sian smiled and continued. "Childhood stories… but once upon a time they were not just for children. They were an important part of a shared history and a shared culture. For hundreds of years, these stories were treated as the truth. And werewolves generally got a bad press. It's almost as if they are hated because they remind us of what we might become without our so-called civilisation. Then there's the whole full moon thing." She laughed. "We're coming up to full moon in the next few days."

Jack smiled. "I'll go and check!" By the light of the candles, he put his boots on loosely and went outside. The cloudless skies of the afternoon had gone, but the moon was indeed visible. Jack remembered the nearly full moon he had seen over Loch Lomond. Now it was fuller still. Surely, only another couple of days and it would be a perfect disc. High up, thin wispy clouds were creeping across the sky, veiling the depths of space. The clouds reflected back some of the moonlight. What were they? Cirrus? Did they precede a change in the weather? Jack wished he'd paid more attention during geography lessons. Not for the first time that day, he mentally crossed his fingers and hoped that the weather would hold.

***

By mid-morning the following day, Sian and Jack had finished the worst of the climb on to Càrn Ban, the mountain behind the bothy. They were nowhere near the summit but had reached a broad ridge. It was comfortable walking, with fine views. To the west, they could look down on the bothy. To the east, there was a circle of cliffs below which was a lochan, reflecting the dull colours of a dull day. Ahead, to the south-east, the mountain rose to its broad summit. The skies, now mostly grey, were still above the tops. Moving along the ridge, the two walkers searched for a good vantage point.

Opposite, on the other side of Coire Mòr, were the crags they had seen the day before. Clinging to a broad scoop between two buttresses was a small area of woodland, perhaps seven hundred metres long. It extended around four hundred metres uphill until it petered out amongst crags too steep and too exposed for trees. Through her camera's zoom lens, Sian could see it was natural forest, not a recent conifer plantation. "That could be really ancient woodland," she said. "It's just a patch, but it's got to have a really complex ecosystem. It would be nice to have a look. It's too high for wild cats, even if they were here, but it's got to have potential for something."

They found an almost completely sheltered spot to sit and made themselves comfortable. It reminded Jack of their previous eeries, and his own sortie into Torridon in July. And rather like those previous occasions, it was uneventful work. For hours, they scanned the landscape, high and low. Sian took some photographs but, unsurprisingly, there was not a wolf to be seen. The clouds deepened in colour and a restless breeze blew in fitful gusts.

Later, they moved further round the lip of the corrie, to where a waterfall plunged off the plateau and tumbled haphazardly down the broken slope. Here, the view of the wood was end on, and half hidden behind a ridge of rock. Again, they sat for what seemed like hours. It's the wrong place, thought Jack, but didn't want to say it out loud. That would be too much like admitting failure.

By three, wisps of cloud began to catch the distant tops. Jack was cold and restless, but also in awe of Sian's capacity to concentrate. She was still looking at the wood, eagle-eyed and attentive to every movement. Keeping his own movement to a minimum, he said: "It's three. We should head down the way we came. I don't like the look of the weather."

Sian said nothing. Jack was about to speak again, but Sian got there first. "OK. But there *is* something there. Might just be a bird, but it's on the ground. I can't quite see what it is." Her camera whirred, taking several shots in automatic succession. Jack raised his binoculars and looked again. Just on the edge of the lower treeline, there *was* movement. But he too couldn't make out what it might be. A mountain hare, possibly? Those were quite large and at this time of year would still have their greyish-brown summer colouring. Again, something moved, and Sian's camera came to life.

"Just can't catch it," she muttered. Then, "There's two of them." The camera clicked again. "But I just can't get a good shot!"

Jack put down his binoculars. "A hare? An arctic fox?" he asked, not daring to voice the idea of wolves.

"Maybe. That might make sense. But not the way they moved. And the arctic fox is extinct in Scotland. There are a few in zoos, but not out here." Still, Sian sat there and looked. Half an hour later she stood up and looked at the sky. "You're right. We'd better go." And that was that. They gathered up their rucksacks, now much lighter today without all their kit, and headed back the way they had come. Half an hour from the bothy, the first drops of rain fell. Not a storm, but large single drops from a gunmetal sky. Anxious not to stop to put on waterproofs, they both increased their speed. By the time they pushed open the door, a short shower had passed them by, to be replaced by a fine drizzle.

Inside, Sian took out her cameras and started to scroll though the images from the day. Most she looked at briefly, then moved on. Towards the end of the sequence, she slowed down and, on each one, carefully zoomed in to examine every pixel of the screen. After several, she put the camera down and rubbed her eyes.

Jack, in the meantime, had made some tea. He handed her a cup.

"Thanks," she said, then put it down and picked up the camera again. "Look at this. Look at the bottom left of the frame. What do you see?"

Jack looked. "Not much. Trees, branches, rocks, broken undergrowth..." He looked again. "Is that on maximum zoom?"

"No. Do that and you literally won't see the wood for the trees. It would all be just pixels. But have a look again when I zoom out." The image expanded. There, between a lichen-covered rock and a branch was the snout of a fox. Only, it wasn't a fox. From the nearby leaves – oak, in the first turn of autumn – he could see it was too big for a fox, and what had Sian said? Arctic foxes were extinct in the wild. And here it was. Admittedly, in nothing like the clear resolution they would have wanted to see, but there it was. A long snout, a dark muzzle, a wide forehead, and the hint in the image, just a hint, of amber where the eyes should be.

"Is it...?" He hardly dared speak.

She did it for him. "Yes. It is. It's the only thing it can be. There are wolves in Scotland – THERE ARE WOLVES IN SCOTLAND!"

***

The rest of the evening passed in a daze. Sian calmly worked through the remaining images. In two more, there was convincing evidence of wolves. In the meantime, Jack cooked a large meal from their combined supplies. They would have to leave tomorrow, and they may as well eat it as much as carry it. And he wanted an early start. The rain had set in. Not heavy, but persistent and he was thinking of the rivers to cross on the way back.

They talked about what to do with their discovery. They agreed immediately not to tell anyone locally. They had to get to a wolf conservancy charity and keep it really quiet. The last thing they wanted was to have locals or amateurs (they laughed – what were they, if not amateurs in this field) ferreting around and ruining everything. Whatever they did, they had to make sure the next steps were careful. They had to make sure the wolves were protected. Somehow, they had survived over two hundred years in secrecy. They couldn't afford to ruin that now.

On top of that, Jack's concern about the rain was well founded. It rained all night and was still raining when they woke in the morning. Streams near the bothy were definitely bigger than the day before. They packed carefully – Sian was doubly careful with her cameras – and donned waterproofs. It was going to be a long walk back.

And so it proved to be. Long, wet and increasingly windy. The path, which soon became a broader track, made for easy walking, especially as it was now mostly downhill. As they trudged along, Jack had the strange feeling they were being watched. He turned round a couple of times but of course there was nothing there. He dismissed it as superstition.

The rivers had changed considerably. Two they forded without concern, but the third was a different story. Where, two days before, water had flowed gently between stepping stones, now it rushed and raged knee-deep or more.

Jack turned to Sian. Against the wind and lashing rain, water running off his nose, he raised his voice.

"Are your socks dry?" Sian nodded. "OK. Take your boots off. Then your socks. Then put your boots back on. Try to keep your socks dry. Cross with your boots on. They'll get wet but you can empty the water out. When we're across, we can put the socks on again. It's a lot better than getting them completely soaked and this is not the time or place to go barefoot."

Sian gave him a quizzical look. "It's OK," he said, "I've done this before. It *does* work. Much better than dripping socks. And…" he grinned, "unbuckle the waist belt on your rucksack, in case you fall in!"

They linked arms and crossed slowly. The torrent tugged at their feet. The water was cold and each step had to be very deliberate. But then they were at the far side and laughing in the rain, emptying their boots back into the river. Their socks would be damp but quite manageable. Shortly, they would be at the bridge and then it would be a couple of hours to the car.

Sian shouted into the wind at Jack, smiling. "I don't know about you, but when we get to Ullapool, I'm heading for the youth hostel, or even a pub. Don't fancy a tent in this!"

The thought cheered them both up. The rain, after all, was only rain. They were damp around the edges, but they'd be warm and dry in a few hours.

On they walked, and coming over the brow of the hill suddenly, through the rain, they could see the Achall valley and Creag Ruadh Lodge. The bridge in front spanned the river as before but the river was now in spate, quite a different creature. Before they got there, and until a short distance from the bridge, the track went through some woods. It gave them some shelter and they were pleased to be out of the wind. Coming out of the trees they could see a vehicle parked near the bridge. It was the Land Rover which had given them the lift.

What happened next was not part of the plan. Sian had stopped to tighten her laces and was a few yards behind Jack. He slowed down as he saw the vehicle, then stopped when he saw the dog. There was the Dobermann, Frodo, alone, wet and looking angry. In the Land Rover was the same driver, clearly about to get out and deal with the dog.

***

He was a moment too late. The dog, "man's best friend", thought Jack to himself, saw Jack and snarled. Still snarling, he charged the fifty feet or so that stood between them. Ten feet away, he launched himself at Jack. Unable to run, Jack brought his arm up in defence, and felt the vicious teeth pierce his waterproof and tear into his arm. The weight of attack sent him staggering back. He felt no pain, just surprise.

Encounters

Whilst deep underground and taking care of the two young wolf cubs, the small wolf pack was extremely busy. The wolves had seen the humans, smelled the human presence but didn't have the feeling of fear this time. An almost maternal or paternal, inexplicable bond between the wolves and humans.

Then a cry of distress, like the cry of a wolf cub calling for its mother, its family, its own wolf pack, bleating and crying in the wilderness. The sounds that permeated the wolf's den were from that very human, in pain, in distress, calling for help.

For the alpha wolf, something moved instinctively and the wolf ran out of the den, above ground and in the direction of the human's cries for help. The agility and speed of the wolf went into full play and in no time at all, the wolf had encountered the human being attacked by a large predator, which the wolf hadn't ever seen before. The wolf, without hesitation, attacked and threw the animal off the human. The great beast was itself much like the wolf and their eyes met. The impenetrable muscle of the wolf, taut and ready to fight, the wolf's jaws fully revealed, eyes transfixed upon the threat, protecting the human cub.

The dog itself looked on in sheer terror at the wolf. The dog had never seen a wolf before. However, this animal was recognisable as a superior force and an adversary that even the Dobermann couldn't fight. The Dobermann, shaking with fear, backed away slowly, then turned and ran, disappearing into the forest and far away.

The wolf looked at the human cub, who was now safe and out of danger. Their eyes met for a fleeting moment and something indescribable but beautiful passed between them before the wolf gently trotted off into the forest. Although it was daylight, the wolf simply ambled back to the den underground where its family was waiting for the alpha to return home safe.

An Amazing Rescue

At the same instant in time, in Jack's eyes, he suddenly saw something twice or three times the size of Frodo flash out of the trees and knock them both flying. There were more snarling teeth and hot breath. The Dobermann let out a weird cry, halfway between a snarl and a yelp. Suddenly, it was the dog who was trying to escape. The other animal threw him to the side like a rag doll and turned towards Jack. For a split second, a wolf looked into the eyes of a human. Had he wanted, he could have placed a paw on the man's shoulder. Then the animal had turned, leaping huge strides into the trees, and was gone.

Jack sat on the track in the rain and looked at his arm. Blood was starting to seep through his clothes. A few metres away, the Dobermann was whimpering. It stood, shocked, wounded, but not apparently seriously injured. Tail between his legs, he ran scared to the bridge, scrabbled up the steps and was gone, heading home to the fireside he had so bravely deserted an hour earlier.

Sian was kneeling beside Jack. "Can you get up?" Then the estate driver was there.

"Are you OK? Can you get to the car? Let's look at that arm. I've got a first aid kit there and we can patch you up 'til you can see a doctor. I'll drive you into Ullapool."

Between them, they helped Jack up. The driver, who had introduced himself as Nick, took Jack's rucksack carefully off his shoulders, mindful not to pull on his arm.

Jack was shaking. "What happened?"

Sian caught his eye and shook her head. Nick grunted. "Let's get you sorted first. Then we can talk about that."

Gently, he helped Jack out of the waterproof and pulled the shirt sleeve up. There was plenty of blood, but that didn't seem to worry him.

Calmly, he aimed an antiseptic spray at the wounds and then expertly wrapped Jack's forearm in a bandage. "Keep your arm up if you can. And lassie," he turned to Sian, "give him something sweet, some chocolate or something, and have some yourself. And I wouldn't mind a bit either. It will help with the shock."

The rain was easing, and Nick busied himself loading the rucksacks into the back of the vehicle. He said nothing more until they had turned round and were driving slowly down the glen. He drove carefully to avoid too many bumps and jolts.

Nick spoke to them both. "Do you know what you saw?"

Sian and Jack nodded. Sian said: "Did you know they were there?"

Nick was quiet for a while as he negotiated a pothole. "Maybe. I'd thought something was there. Now we know. And there must be more. What are you going to do? Whatever your plans, you've got a big responsibility."

Jack, in the back, nursed his arm as they drove along. He didn't listen in detail, but Sian had obviously decided it would be easier to explain the whole story. Nick seemed to agree with their plan.

"For my part," he said, "I'd rather my new boss didn't get on his high horse about this. I'll not lie to him, but I'm not going to tell the whole story just yet. It'll be best if there are some experts involved first. Hopefully, he'll see the PR angle and do the right thing."

***

Much later, when Nick had persuaded the GP to see Jack, when the wounds had been cleaned and a couple of stitches put in, Nick and Sian collected Jack's car and they found rooms for Jack and Sian at The Ferry Boat Inn.

The three of them sat in a quiet corner of the bar. Jack had his arm in a sling and felt sore and clumsy. Sian showed Nick the few images of the wolves in the trees. He spoke little, but nodded as Sian explained what they had found out.

"Well," he said, "I agree. It's good we know they're there. It makes sense. It has obviously been them predating the deer, and for a while, too. In fact, for hundreds of years. In some of the quieter glens, the trees are doing better than you'd expect with so many deer around. The wolves must be keeping them on the move. And there must be more than one pack, so they can't be in this area alone."

He paused, as if wondering how to capture his thoughts, so many ideas all at once. "The next challenge is to keep them there safely. It's got the potential to revolutionise land management in this part of the world, but only if we don't interfere more than we have to. They'll be plenty of naysayers, so your friends in the conservation world will need to get busy. Here's my number."

Jack and Sian gave him their numbers in return and they all promised to keep in touch. Nick left them a little later, and Jack made his way to his room. He was tired, and he needed a bit of genuine peace and quiet. The room looked out over the harbour and along Loch Broom. The mountains of their recent adventures were visible in the distance. One-handed, he opened the window and moved a chair so he could sit and admire the view. Dusk was falling and the skies had cleared. There was barely a breath of wind and Jack could feel the cool air of autumn as it seemed to settle calmly over the hills and water. The moon, now a full circle hanging in the sky, shed its reflected light over the town. There was hardly a sound.

Epilogue

The wolf family all slowly emerged one by one from the underground den and cave that had been their home for many generations. Many generations of wolves that had never set foot above ground and never howled or alerted any humans to their presence. This subterranean realm had now become a bridge between worlds. On that bridge had now met two other worlds. The world of the humans and the world of Britain's wild wolves had met for the first time in centuries – a very different encounter to times of olden days. What will this new world bring? The forests are back, the abodes and kingdoms that the wolves naturally live in are also here. There was fear and there was excitement; now it was time.

The alpha wolf then became still and, transfixed in the moonlight, tilted his head back, gazed at the moon, the night sky and the darkened forests and landscape around, and gave a majestic wolf howl, which was very quickly joined in by the omega and members of the tiny wolf pack. Their presence was no longer a secret.

***

Jack sat looking out of the window into the night sky deep in thought about what he had experienced, felt and seen, haunted by the amazing beauty of what happened. Musing and smiling, Jack thought, "but who would believe it?". The moon looked almost like an old galleon being thrown around in a dark mysterious sea. A dog nearby barked; Jack smiled again. Then, in the distance, there was a different music entirely. A long howl. First one, then another in answer. A strange and mysterious call, part melancholy, part tribal clamour. A call from the wild and a call of the wild; a call to the moon, a sound etched into generations of legend.

The howl of the wolf was loud and clear, penetrating the seemingly once impenetrable night, heard far and wide across the landscape of the United Kingdom.

Addendum and References

Thank you for reading this book and I hope you enjoyed the story; whilst the story itself and characters are works of fiction, the various settings, subject matter and issues are very real and relevant to all of somehow.

For this reason, I attach this addendum and reference section for anyone who wishes to find out more about any of these issues and topics covered in this book.

The list of organisations here does not represent a complete list of those people and organisations who work in these areas. Those referenced here include those who have actively cooperated, provided support, knowledge and information, those who have chosen and agreed to include their contact details, and others that I am a member or affiliate member of and been introduced to. There is a lot of overlap and cooperation in their respective and shared mission goals and values. The addendum format is a standard one, a basic list of contact details including websites and other such contacts and references. All the information shared here and contact information for the various organisations is also all available for the public record. Thank you.

The author's own website details are Dave Gregson Writes and Important To IMportant For Dave Gregson Writes https://davegregson.co.uk/

Dave Gregson is a writer of both adult and children's fiction and has also published his autobiography, focused on school and workplace bullying, with proceeds going to charity.
davegregson.co.uk

Autistic Inclusive Meets (AIM)
A truly inclusive autism association, "we provide support and advice to families and individuals, promote acceptance of autism through education of the general public, and protect autistic rights by campaigning against autistic mistreatment".
https://autisticinclusivemeets.org/

Bullies Out https://bulliesout.com/
T109 Titan House, Cardiff Bay Business Centre, Lewis Road, Cardiff, CF24 5BS. Office number (not helpline), 029 2049 2169. For those needing help, please contact our mentors here https://bulliesout.com/what-we-do/e-mentoring/

Carers UK
https://www.carersuk.org/

The Ben Kinsella Trust
"No family or community should suffer the loss of a life to knife crime".
https://benkinsella.org.uk/

The Conduct Change Foundation
Advocacy, campaigning, education and awareness raising about workplace bullying.
https://www.conductchangefoundation.org/, info@conductchangefoundation.org, Founder Nicki Eyre 07921264921

National Autistic Society
The UK's leading charity for people on the autism spectrum and their families. Since 1962, the charity has been providing support, guidance

and advice, as well as opportunities to help create a society that works for autistic people.
www.autism.org.uk/, nas@nas.org.uk

NSPCC
https://www.nspcc.org.uk/, full contact details on the website, helpline 0808 800 5000, help@nspcc.org.uk

The Samaritans
https://www.samaritans.org/ call for free 116 123

Survivors UK
https://www.survivorsuk.org/

The Jordan legacy
A society that acknowledges, supports, and advocates for men and non-binary people who have been affected by rape or sexual abuse.
"practical actions to make our communities and workplaces mentally healthy and psychologically safe places".
https://thejordanlegacy.com/, hello@thejordanlegacy.com,

Alladale Wilderness Reserve
https://alladale.com, hospitality@alladale.com, Ardgay, IV24 3BS, 01863 755338

ACEVO (Association of chief Executives for Voluntary Organisations)
https://www.acevo.org.uk/

Big Picture Scotland and the Scottish Rewilding Alliance
https://www.scotlandbigpicture.com, office@scotlandbigpicture.com,
Press and Media Peter Cairns, peter@scotlandbigpicture.com, 07816774431
https://www.rewild.scot/

Badgers Trust

https://www.badgertrust.org.uk

Bat conservation Trust and National Bat Helpline
https://www.bats.org.uk

If you have found a bat in need of rescue or need to report a bat crime:

Please call us as a matter of urgency on 0345 1300 228 so we can advise you. The Helpline operates from 9.30 a.m.–4.30 p.m. Monday to Friday. If your enquiry is outside of these times or you cannot be connected, please visit our website without delay for advice on what to do.

• Found a bat: https://www.bats.org.uk/advice/help-ive-found-a-bat

• If you are a vet or wildlife hospital who have had a bat brought in: https://www.bats.org.uk/advice/a-bat-has-been-brought-to-our-veterinary-surgery

Bat crime: https://www.bats.org.uk/advice/bats-and-the-law/reporting-bat-crimes

Born Free Foundation
UK, https://www.bornfree.org.uk/, online enquiry form, 01403 240 170, UK Office, 2nd floor, Frazel House, 14 Carfax, Horsham, West Sussex, RH12 1ER

British Hedgehog Preservation Society
https://www.britishhedgehoghogs.org.uk/ info@britishhedgehogs.org.uk, 01584 890801, Hedgehog House, Dhustone, Ludlow, Shropshire, SY8 3PL

British Big Cat Society
sightings@britishbigcats.org, 01752 251153, PO Box 28. Plymouth, Devon, PL1 1AA

Buglife
https://www.buglife.org.uk , info@buglife.org.uk,

Cats Protection League
https://www.cats.org.uk/

The Conservation Volunteers (TCV)
https://www.tcv.org.uk/, information@tcv.org.uk, 01302 388 883

Folklore Society
https://folklore-society.com/

Forest of Dean Historical Society
https://www.forestofdeanhistory.org.uk/

League Against Cruel Sports
https://www.league.org.uk
info@league.org.uk. 01483 524 250. New Sparling House, Holloway Hill, Godalming, Surrey, QU7 1QZ

Mammal Society
https://www.mammal.org.uk

National Park UK
https://nationalparks.uk/

National Trust
https://www.nationaltrust.org.uk

NatureScot
https://www.nature.scot/, ENQUIRIES@nature.scot, Great Glen House, Leachkin Road, Inverness, IV3 BNW, 01463 725 000

NCVO (National Council for Voluntary Organisations)
https://www.ncvo.org.uk/

Open Country
Supporting those with disabilities and accessibility needs to access the countryside, with support and volunteering for many countryside and wildlife projects.
https://www.opencountry.org.uk/, info@opencountry.org.uk
Community House, 46 East Parade, Harrogate, North Yorkshire, HG1 5LY, 01423 507227

The Owls Trust
https://theowlstrust.org/ , info@theowlstrust.org,
North Wales Bird Trust, Bodafon Farm Park, Llandudno, LL30 3BB, 01492 870719, 07776416922

People's Trust for Endangered Species
https://ptes.org/

Ramblers UK
https://ramblers.org.uk/

Amphibians and Reptiles Conservation Trust (ARC)
https://www.arc-trust.org/, enquiries@arc-trust.org, 744 Christchurch Road, Boscombe, Bournemouth, BH7 6BZ, 01202 391319

Red Kite Alliance
https://www.redkite.alliance.co.uk/

RSPCA
https://www.rspca.org.uk

RSPB
https://www.rspb.org.uk/

Royal Zoological Society of Scotland
https://www.rzss.org.uk

Rewilding Britain
https://www.rewildingbritain.org.uk/ , info@rewildingbritain.org.uk

Saving Wildcats
https://savingwildcats.org.uk/ , wildcats@rzss.org.uk, 0131 314 0380

Save Me Trust
https://savemetrust.co.uk/

St George's Crypt
https://www.stgeorgescrypt.org.uk/

Wildwood Trust
https://wildwoodtrust.org/ , info@wildwoodtrust.org, 01227 712 111, Herne Common, Herne Bay, Kent, CT6 7LQ

Woodland Trust
https://www.woodlandtrust.org.uk/

Wolf Watch UK
https://wolfwatch.uk/, info@wolfwatch.uk

Yorkshire Wildlife Trust and the Wildlife Trusts
https://www.ywt.org.uk/, info@ywt.org.uk, 1 St Georges Place, York, Yo24 1GN, 01904 659570
https://www.wildlifetrusts.org/

VisitBritain
https://www.visitbritain.com/

VisitScotland
https://www.visitscotland.com/

Vincent Wildlife Trust
https://www.vwt.org.uk

Voluntary Action Leeds
https://www.valyouleeds.co.uk/, valyou@val.org.uk, Stringer House, 34 Lupton Street, Hunslet, Leeds, Ls10 2QW, 0113 297 7920

A picture of a wolf which I have adopted and lives in the reserve at the Wildwood Trust.